DARK
COGNITIONS

Kimberlee Mendoza

DARK COGNITIONS

Contact Information: titleadmin@pelicanbookgroup.com

All scripture quotations, unless otherwise indicated, are taken from the Holy Bible, New International Version(R) NIV(R) Copyright 1973, 1978, 1984, 2011 by Biblica, Inc.™ Used by permission of Zondervan. All rights reserved worldwide. www.zondervan.com

Cover Art by *Nicola Martinez*
Harbourlight Books, a division of Pelican Ventures, LLC
www.pelicanbookgroup.com PO Box 1738 *Aztec, NM * 87410

Harbourlight Books sail and mast logo is a trademark of Pelican Ventures, LLC

Publishing History
First Harbourlight Edition, 2014
Paperback Edition ISBN 978-1-61116-358-2
Electronic Edition ISBN 978-1-61116-357-5
Published in the United States of America

Dedication

To my mother, Ruth Porter, my biggest fan and a big reason I am who I am. I love you, Mom!

Praise

If you think you've got the plot figured out, think again. Mendoza writes with the mind of a chess champion. She's always at least three moves ahead of her reader ~ Paul McShane, Good News, Etc.

Ms. Mendoza shows the reality of life, with trials and heartache, through her characters giving them a highly believable quality that her readers will remember long after they read the last page~ Bluegrass Romance Reviews

Prologue

The rhythmic sound of the tapping pencil had a hypnotic effect. Dr. Raven's eyes started to glaze over and his brain with it. The phone rang, jolting him back. Tossing the pencil in its cup, he answered the phone. "Yes?"

"Your new patient, Dr. Manifold, is here to see you."

"Send him in."

Dr. Brian Manifold entered the dim counseling office and stood in the shadow of a bookcase.

Raven treated patients like Manifold every day. Something he took pride in—his ability to read a client, and by the slumped manner in which Manifold carried his broad shoulders, Raven could tell that this once successful doctor was now a broken man.

Manifold was dressed well enough; gray suit, black tie, and his brown, slightly gray-salted hair neatly combed to one side. His beard looked to be freshly trimmed and his horn-rimmed glasses seemingly free from smudges. To the naked eye, one might think this man had it together. But the morose expression in Brian's eyes told the real story.

"Hello, doctor. Please be seated." Raven waved to a leather chair to the side of his desk, and then straightened his yellow tie. "Can I get you something to drink? Water? Coffee, perhaps?"

Dr. Manifold shook his head as he slowly peered

around the room, dazed.

"Well then, I guess we'll just get started." Raven withdrew a legal pad from his top drawer.

"I'm not sure why I am here," Manifold whispered. "Dr. Jensen told me this morning you wanted to see me, but honestly, I don't know what all the fuss is about."

"We'll get to that in a minute, but first I need you to sit down."

The man didn't budge. "Please, call me Brian."

"I'm not here to be your friend, doctor. I'm here to determine if you're still fit to practice psychology. Now, I'll ask again. Will you please sit down?"

Like a child ordered to his room, Manifold scuffled to the couch and positioned himself on the edge. His gaze then fell to the multi-colored carpet.

This wouldn't be easy, but that was part of the fun—the challenge. Raven sat in the chair opposite the couch and picked up a file from the coffee table. "I have to admit, I'm quite surprised to find you on my calendar today."

Manifold folded his arms and offered a tight smile. "You, too?"

Raven stared at him for a moment before opening the folder in his lap. "I see that you came to St. Ruth's Hospital at the top of your class. Until a few months ago, you were one of the best doctors we had on our staff." Raven peered over the top of his bifocals. "Which brings me to your visit. What happened? Why are you here?"

The once "great doctor" shifted in his seat, and tugged at his collar. "I'm not sure what you mean."

Here we go. Raven lifted the file in the air to emphasize his point. "It says here that you've been late almost every day for the past few months. There have been several complaints of yelling coming from your office, usually when you're alone. And most recently, you have been accused of drinking on the job." He laid the report back in his lap and leaned forward, emphasizing each word as a teacher might do to a child. "I repeat, Dr. Manifold. What happened to you?"

"Things have been difficult at home," he rasped before his gaze fell back to the carpet.

The air grew still, and the grandfather clock in the corner ticked like a drone in a metal factory.

Raven removed his glasses and rubbed his eyes. "Is that it, doctor?"

Brian shrugged.

"Are you aware that I hold the power to revoke your license? That the hospital board looks to my recommendation to determine your fate? According to my report, your actions have raised a few concerns. And in our business, it's a problem when the counselor exhibits more aberrant behavior than his patients."

"I don't know what you want from me."

"How about the truth? How about sharing what's going on in that head of yours? You're in a lot of trouble, doctor, and I'm the only one who can help you now. Either you're honest with me, or you're through." He tossed the file on the table by his chair, the papers fluttering to rest. "Now, what's going on?"

Manifold folded his arms and pursed his lips, his expression as cold as a day old corpse.

Raven sighed. He wanted to help this man, but he could only help someone who wanted it. Reaching for the file, he shifted to stand.

"OK." Manifold blinked, eased himself into the couch, and then closed his eyes. "But what you're asking me to do is not going to be easy. Things are happening that are way beyond my explanation. I've been living it for months, and I don't even remotely understand what's going on myself." He cleared his throat. "Coffee."

Raven titled his head to the side. "I'm sorry?"

"I'll take some coffee."

"Yes, of course," he said. Raven crossed to a brewed pot and poured a cup. "Sugar or cream?"

"Black, please."

He nodded and handed Manifold the foam container. "Please continue."

"Time is a funny thing. To some, it's what they see. A man may notice gray hair and wrinkles taking over his once smooth complexion. A woman may notice her child developing into an adult. Both may realize their pets will soon die. For me, I feel lost in some void. As if time doesn't exist."

"And why's that?"

"I wish I knew." He stared into his cup.

"And why do you suppose you don't know?" Raven sat back in his chair.

"It's all a blur." Manifold seemed mesmerized by the coffee's rising steam.

"Well, why don't you start from what you do know?"

The man finally seemed to relax against the couch cushion, apparently ready to comply.

1

Danielle flipped on a desk lamp and walked behind the desk. The office felt still, just as she liked it. But the peace wouldn't last. The rest of the staff would be along soon to start another—

An explosive blast shattered the quiet.

Her heart lurched as she dropped to the floor. *What was that?* She listened hard in the soft light, afraid to stand. Silence rang in her ears. Slowly, she stood and inched out from behind her desk.

A single light glowed from under Dr. Manifold's door. Did she dare go down there? She eyed the elevator and then her purse. Leaving the building seemed better. But what if he was hurt? Compassion— or maybe curiosity—won out. On tiptoes, she crept forward, her rubber soles squeaking on the tile floor.

"Hello? Dr. Manifold? Are you in there?" Her heart hammered. She lifted a hand to the door, and then closed it in a fist, hesitant to discover what lay within.

The receptionist's telephone echoed down the dark hallway, almost sending her into cardiac arrest. Swallowing, she pushed the door. "Dr. Manifold? Brian?"

A groan sounded from behind the couch.

She leaned forward, keeping her feet planted.

A lock of the doctor's brown hair was draped across the arm of the couch.

"Dr. Manifold, are you OK?" She stepped around the couch and stared in horror.

A diminutive crimson river flowed from the doctor's ear, and a gun hung loosely from his hand.

Timidly, she grabbed the weapon and tossed it into a nearby chair, then pulled off her sweater and pressed it against his wound, before checking his pulse with her free hand. *Weak.*

She pulled her cell phone out. Unable to remember the direct line to the ER on the bottom floor, she dialed the shack below. "Security?" Danielle yelled once someone answered. "Hurry and get up here! Dr. Manifold shot himself!"

In what seemed like hours, two security guards armed with only nightsticks and brawn bolted through the office door.

"What happened?" Bernie, the older of the two guards, ran over and knelt next to them.

"I heard a gunshot." Her lip quivered. She blinked back tears and pointed to the nearby chair. "The gun is there."

The guard lifted his radio. "Mac, get someone in ER to bring up a gurney. We have an injured man and shots fired."

The radio squawked. "Say again."

"Bring a gurney from ER. One of the doctors has been shot!"

"Yes, sir."

The other guard, Les, peeked over the couch with one eyebrow raised. Instantly, his face became grass green. He bolted for a trashcan by the door and expelled the contents of his stomach.

Dani grimaced.

"Les, why don't you check the other offices?"

Bernie asked.

The man nodded without saying a word and stepped into the hallway.

Danielle wanted to join him. Nausea fluttered through her stomach, as well.

"Did you see what happened?" Bernie searched her face.

She shook her head, her gaze lingering on the doorway. "I just heard the shot, and found him with the gun."

"I see." He nodded and put a couple fingers to the inert man's neck. "His pulse is weak."

An elevator bell chimed in the hallway and clear relief crossed the guard's face.

Hers, too, she was sure. It took everything in her not to bolt. It wasn't as if she'd never seen blood before. But this was Brian—her colleague, and once, a friend.

Les entered. "All clear."

Two medical personnel entered with a gurney.

Danielle stood and stared at her scarlet hands. "May I go home?"

"I'm sorry. Not yet." Bernie offered a tight smile. "The cops will want to talk to you. Why don't you go with Les to the ER waiting room, and I'll let the police know that you're there." He faced his partner. "Let her clean up and get some coffee. And wipe your face." Bernie motioned his hand over his own face in rapid circles. "You've got stuff, um… "

"Yes, sir." Les wiped at his face with the back of his brown sleeve. "I'm sorry, sir. I've just never seen anything like this."

"No worries, son. It's your first week." Bernie patted Les's back. "Just take care of the lady, OK? I'll work this out."

Les nodded and faced her. "Come on, miss."

God help Brian. Right now, it didn't matter that he'd been a jerk; Danielle didn't want him to die.

2

Three Months Earlier

Danielle hung up the phone and glanced over the counter. Her boss, Merle approached.

"Can I see you a moment?" Merle's expression was unusually stern. She didn't wait for Danielle's answer; she spun around and headed for the conference room.

"Sure." Danielle swallowed as she followed.

"Sit down, please."

Danielle slid into one of the high-backed chairs, toying with her thumb ring. She wracked her brain trying to remember what she might have done to get fired.

"I'll get straight to the point. Are you seeing Dr. Manifold?"

Her heart skipped. She wished. "Not really. I mean, he's shown interest, but we haven't gone out or anything."

"Do you make a habit of dating married men?"

Danielle's chest heaved. "Married?"

Merle stared at Danielle before responding. "Yes. He has a wife named Rhonda. Surely you knew that."

Danielle suddenly felt sick. "We've never gone out. I'm a Christian woman. I would never…" Her eyes welled with tears. She didn't know if it was because she was embarrassed, angry, hurt, or ashamed. She'd never look at Brian—Dr. Manifold—the same way again. "I'm sorry. I didn't know."

"I'm glad to hear your intentions weren't depraved. Rhonda is my friend, and..." Merle stood and moved to the door. "I like you, Ms. Tyler. You're a great assistant. I'd like to see you stay."

Danielle stood on wobbly legs and tried to offer a smile. "And I'd like to, ma'am."

Her boss nodded and left.

Danielle's confused thoughts zeroed in one thing. Brian's advances. She'd actually been planning to accept his next invitation to lunch. *What a jerk! Married?*

⊰∘⊱

The clock on the table by his bedside table read 7:00 AM. Brian gazed at the blinking red colon and groaned.

The hum of his wife's breathing matched the blinking of the colon.

He squeezed his eyes shut and focused on the clock again. 7:01 AM. Brian flopped onto his back and looked at the ceiling. A small crack cut through the blown popcorn. He flexed his toes under the covers, not wanting to face the clock again. Work wasn't for another hour. Brian turned toward his wife.

Her mouth hung slightly open and hair draped down over her face.

He nudged her shoulder.

She didn't budge.

"Rhonda," he whispered.

Still no movement.

"Rhonda, wake up."

Nothing.

Brian shook his head and faced back to the clock. 7:03.

Close enough. He got out of bed, dressed, and then headed for the kitchen. He stopped in the doorway and smiled.

His ten-year-old daughter sat perched on the edge of the sink, in yellow daisy pajamas, an open white robe, and hot pink slippers, looking like an angel. Her focus seemed drawn to something out the window. Beams of sunlight kissed her hair, causing her honey-blonde tresses to sparkle. How quickly she'd grown. At this point, she was all he had.

Lara reached into the whitewashed cupboard, grabbed a cup and filled it with water. Through the bottom of her glass, she must have spotted her father. She jumped. Water splashed down.

"Dad!" She frowned at the droplets that covered her pajamas. "Look what you've made me do!"

"Sorry." He chuckled and handed her a dishtowel.

She grabbed it and rubbed the front of her top. "What are you doing, anyway?"

"Nothing. Just thinking about how proud you make me."

"Why?" She glared at him with slight irritation. "I'm only drinking water."

"You're a good kid. What can I say?" He pulled a tan coffee mug from the cabinet. "And I'm amazed at how much you look like your mother did." He grinned and faced her.

She hopped off the counter and crossed her arms. "You act like mom's dead, when she's only asleep in the other room."

"Of course she is." He turned away and poured himself a cup of coffee. "She's *always* asleep."

"Dad, please don't get mad at me for saying this." She took a deep breath. "But it's your fault she doesn't get better."

"Don't start." Brian stared at the microwave. He couldn't look at his daughter. Mainly, because she wasn't far off.

"But Dad, if you'd just talk to her, then maybe things would change."

He didn't have the energy to fight her about this again. "I need to get to work."

Lara stepped forward with her arms out. "I love you, Daddy."

Brian hugged her and kissed the top of her head. "And I love you, too, sweetheart."

"The bus will be here soon, so I'd better get ready." She pulled away and walked down the hallway, but spun back. "Dad, just to let you know, we're having Parents' Night at school next Friday. I hope you'll go."

"I wouldn't miss it." He finished off the last drop of coffee, walked to the master bedroom and nudged the door open.

Across the room lay his wife. Her eyes were open, but distant. Her hair was matted to her head, and her once rosy cheeks were now hollow and gray.

How he missed her. "I'll be home late."

She didn't stir.

"Goodbye." Brian closed the door and walked toward the entryway. He glanced back at his room and shook his head. He would go to work. That would be enough for now.

Danielle spent weeks washing any feelings of Brian out of her head. The whole idea of her crunching on a married man gave her the willies. But now someone else held her interest. And this time, she confirmed that he was single from several sources.

Peeking around a computer monitor, Danielle watched Dr. Ray Jensen as he talked to one of the residents. *He is so gorgeous.* Tall, dark messy hair, high cheekbones, and the most gorgeous gray-blue eyes. Every time he looked at her, she melted in her ugly white shoes.

But she was nothing more than an assistant. Though he'd always been nice, he kept a healthy distance. Or maybe the rumors about her were too much for him. Chasing after Dr. Brian Manifold did little for her reputation. How was she supposed to know he was married? No one seemed to notice that she put on the brakes the minute she found out. Now the rumors were rampant, the damage done. And it didn't help that Brian still flirted with her in front of everyone.

"Danielle?"

She blinked.

Merle waved a hand in front of her face.

"Sorry. I guess I zoned out for a second. These double shifts are killers." Danielle yawned.

"Well, medical school is terrible compared to double shifts, I've heard. Being a resident is worse than anything." Merle handed over a stack of files and rubbed her swollen torso. "If you'll take these up to the seventh floor that would be great. I need to get off my feet and feed the little one a piece of that chocolate ice cream cake left from Dr. Benton's birthday party."

"Wouldn't you be better eating prenatal vitamins

and spinach instead?"

Merle laughed. "I wouldn't eat spinach even if I wasn't pregnant. But I'll be sure to sprinkle some vitamins, and maybe some carrots, on top."

Danielle wrinkled her nose. "And I bet ice cream manufacturers will be knocking down your door to get that recipe. Sounds yummy." She settled the files in the crook of her elbow. "I'd be happy to take these up."

Merle lumbered toward the break room.

Danielle checked Ray's current location. He stood poised at the elevator, waiting for the door to open.

She walked next to him but didn't say anything.

The elevator dinged and the door slid open.

Ray walked in first and turned to face the numbered buttons. He punched seven, glanced at her, and then grinned. "Floor?"

"The same, please."

He nodded.

The door closed and only the melodic tune of a country-western cheatin' song played in the space. Her heart fluttered. She took a deep breath and prayed Ray didn't know this song.

He shifted his weight from one foot to another. His spicy aftershave tickled her nose, and her stomach flipped. Why couldn't she just tell him how she felt? *Because I can't take the thought of him rejecting me.*

The elevator reached its floor and opened.

He motioned for her to go first.

"Thanks." She stepped out, disappointed.

"Have a good day," he said, his gray eyes twinkling at her as he walked toward the counseling offices.

Her voice caught, leaving her without a response. *You, too. Hope you have a nice day. You're beautiful. Marry me.* She pinched her eyes closed. If her hands weren't filled with files, she'd probably slap herself.

"Are you OK?" Ray's voice startled her.

Her eyes shot wide open.

He stood close enough for her to smell his spicy cologne again. It made her heart flutter.

She gulped. "Um, yeah. Double shift. Just tired."

He lightly touched her shoulder. "Maybe you should take a break. I'd hate to see you pass out in the hall."

She nodded dumbly.

"Where are you going with those?"

"These?" *Snap out of it.* "Oh, the files. Right. Um, just here." She walked to the counter and handed them to the receptionist. "Merle said you needed these."

The woman nodded, took them, and turned away.

"You sure you're OK? Maybe you should lie down." Ray stepped to her side.

"I'm just hungry, I missed my lunch." And before she could stop herself, "You could join me." Her heart leapt into her throat.

He stared at her, and then checked his watch. "Yeah, I suppose. It's almost dinner time."

"I hear the cafeteria is serving potato cheese soup today."

"Oh?" His cell phone rang. He held up a finger as he checked the display. "Um, just give me a second. I need to take this call."

"Sure."

He stepped a few feet away.

She watched him with fascination. Would he really go to lunch with her? Her stomach flipped. She needed someone like him in her life. Everything she'd heard about him said he was worth knowing — a

Christian man with strong morals and a good sense of humor; the kind of man she had been praying for since she was young enough to care.

A second later, he snapped his phone closed and walked back to her. "I'm sorry, but I can't today. How about tomorrow?"

"That would be great." She offered a grin and nodded. Anything more and she'd give herself away.

"OK, then." He waved and walked toward his office.

She crossed to the elevator and stepped inside. When the door closed, she clapped a hand over her mouth to hold in a triumphant scream.

Remembering the cameras, she looked up into the glass dome in the corner and mouthed, "I have a date with Dr. Ray, Bernie!" She pumped her fist in victory.

3

Dr. Brian Manifold squealed his expensive silver sedan into the parking space that bore his name and braked hard. He threw open the door, slammed it, and then braced himself to enter the four-story hospital that he called "home."

An all-too-familiar pain shot through the pit of his stomach and he took a deep breath, willing it to stop. Thinking about personal issues was something he didn't do. He couldn't do. Not and stay sane.

The elevator door opened and his pain subsided when he caught sight of Danielle. Her smile remained the only drug that numbed him from reality.

A blonde curl escaped from her hair clip, and cornflower blue eyes pulled him in like a pool on a summer day. He started towards her.

Ray stepped out of the other elevator and walked up to him.

Brian sighed. "What do you need, Ray?"

"Remember we have a meeting tomorrow morning." Ray's expression and tone were serious. "I advise you not miss it this time. I can't keep covering for you."

"Nice to see you, too."

Brian glanced over Ray's shoulder and winked at Danielle.

She dropped her gaze to some charts on the counter.

Ray followed his gaze. "Look, I know things aren't good at home. Maybe you need to take a break. Spend some time with Rhonda."

Brian's gaze snapped to Ray's. *Home?* He couldn't do that. "No, I'm fine. I'd rather work."

"We're friends, right?"

No. Not really. Once his best friend, Ray had managed to "apple-polish" his way to the top, and Brian despised him for it. "Sure. Once upon a time. Well, until you moved into management." *And climbed over my back to get there.*

"I don't think that's what ruined our friendship, Brian." Ray took a step forward. "I think it was the accident. And the sooner we talk—"

Brian pressed his lips together and pushed past Ray in the direction of his office. They weren't going to talk about this. Not here. Not anywhere. Never. It was none of Ray's business. They weren't friends anymore. They had nothing to say.

Ray matched his pace. "I may be management, but I'm still a psychiatrist. We both know the importance of talking things out. And trust me, friend, you need it."

"I'm fine." Brian reached into his pocket and took out his keys.

"Are you?"

Brian glared at him and shoved the key in the lock.

Ray grabbed his arm. "Look man, I know things are different for you. Rhonda used to be your world and now you're lost."

Brian shook his arm free and stepped into the dark room. He felt along the wall, looking for the switch. "It's hard to love a vegetable," Brian mumbled, snapping the light on. "I'm not saying I don't love her,

18

but we're growing apart." He swung his briefcase on the desk and snapped it open.

Ray stepped behind a high backed chair and fingered the top. "Don't blow it, man. You need to talk to her."

"What am I blowing?"

Ray came around the chair and rested on the edge of the couch with his arms crossed. "It's obvious you're trying to start something with Danielle."

"Danielle?" Brian's stomach flipped at the mention of her name, but he managed to sound surprised. He couldn't deny the way she made him feel.

Ray eyed him.

Brian tried to stare him down.

His boss didn't budge.

"Yeah, so? What's a little flirting? It's harmless. I promise." Brian busied himself with the files in his briefcase. *Go away, I beg you.*

Ray stepped forward. "Is it?"

Brian rolled his eyes and met Ray's stare. "Listen, Ray. Our friendship isn't like it used to be. You don't know me anymore. I don't owe you an explanation." He closed the briefcase and set it on the floor. "There are things in my life...look, you couldn't possibly understand what I'm dealing with."

"That's why I'm here. To help you sort a few things out. I'm worried about you." He walked to the edge of the desk. "I really am sorry about taking the management job. I know it caught you off guard. Maybe if I'd known it would ruin our friendship, I would have reconsidered."

Brian looked up, but didn't respond. Though he hated to admit it, pride would not allow their friendship to continue and that made him angry.

"Come on, man. Let's get past this and let me help you," Ray said. "So what if things are different. It's all material. I'm still here for you."

Brian heard the words, but they were meaningless, ringing hollow to his ears. Brian rolled his shoulders back, unable to accept Ray's offering. "You're my boss, Ray, not my friend."

Ray pressed his lips together and nodded. "I'm sorry you feel that way."

"Yeah, like you said, things are different." Brian turned his attention to his cell phone. "If you'll excuse me, I have a client coming soon, and I need to return some calls first."

"Very well, I'll go. But whether it's me or someone else you talk to, you need to get help." Ray crossed to the door and turned back. "I know you a lot better than you're willing to admit. You're losing the battle with your marriage, and with God."

Brian blinked. "God? I'm not at war with God, because I don't believe there is a God."

The impact of that statement was clear on Ray's face. A verbal punch to his old friend's psyche, for sure. Brian tried not to gloat.

"I'm praying for you, Brian."

"You can go now." If he let Ray in even a little bit, he'd never leave.

Ray sighed, and finally left.

Brian glowered at the empty doorway. The pain in his gut returned. Holding his stomach, he slumped in his seat. *I should cancel my next appointment.* He started to push the intercom, when a gorgeous brunette sauntered in. Something about the way she looked at him made Brian think that they'd met before.

The woman smiled. "I'm Kristina Stephens. My

friends call me Krissy. I'm your two o'clock."

Brian glanced down at his calendar and cleared his throat. "Yes, of course. Come in and have a seat."

She glided across the brown Berber carpet like a fashion model on a runway. She eased onto the couch.

Brian swallowed and reached for a pad of paper. His hand trembled. He pushed it against the desktop. *Get hold of yourself. This is absurd. I'm a professional.* He took a deep breath, grabbed the paper and moved to sit across from her.

He smiled and waited for her to speak. When she remained silent, he said, "So tell me, Ms. Stephens, why have you sought counseling?"

A small tear slid down her cheek and made a line in her makeup. "I'm scared for my life. A man's been calling my cell phone, almost daily, threatening to kill me."

Brian frowned. "Have you contacted the police?"

She shook her head. "I've tried, but it hasn't done any good."

"I see." Brian couldn't shake the feeling that he'd seen this woman before. Her presence triggered emotions he couldn't explain. Sympathy. Sorrow. Passion. "Take your time." He handed her a tissue.

"No one believes me. They all think I'm crazy." She dabbed at her face.

He'd had many cases like hers before, young girls seeking attention because they weren't getting it from someone else. One teenage girl even went to the point of sending herself black roses and a dead animal carcass just to get her parents to notice her.

The woman before him couldn't be more than twenty years old. It was beyond him why she'd have to work to get anyone's attention. She was gorgeous.

"And why do you think no one believes you?"

"Because I have no evidence." She sniffed.

"But you're sure someone is stalking you?"

"Positive."

"I see." Brian wrote some comments on his pad.

Her almond eyes seemingly searched his face. "You don't believe me?"

He met her gaze. "I didn't say that. I simply want to hear your side of it."

"I told you all there is to tell."

"Why do you think someone is stalking you?"

She shrugged. "I just feel someone with me all the time."

"Have you seen anyone?"

She shook her head. "No, just a feeling."

Brian cocked his head and grinned. "Let me ask you something, Ms. Stephens. Are you married?"

A playful smiled crossed her face. "No, are you?"

"Boyfriend?" he asked.

"Not anymore."

She reached inside her taffy-colored handbag and pulled out a red tin. While keeping her eyes focused on Brian, she slowly opened the case, placed a white candy on her tongue, and methodically brought it into her mouth.

Brian loosed his tie a bit. "How do you feel about him now?"

"I still love him."

"And did he leave you?"

She laughed.

"Did I say something amusing?"

She tossed her hair back over her on shoulder, leaned forward, and stared at him through her eyelashes. "Men don't leave *me*, doctor. I leave *them*."

Brian nodded once. "I see." He scribbled this remark. "So, you loved him, but felt a need to leave him?"

Krissy snapped the tin closed and tossed it in her purse. "Can we get off this and back to the reason I came here?"

"No." Brian shook his head. "I think your ex-boyfriend could be a part of why you're here. I think it would be good for you to talk about it."

"Look, I assure you, my ex has nothing to do with that."

"Have you ever considered that he could be the one harassing you?"

She cocked her head to the side. "Not likely."

"And why's that?"

Krissy rolled her eyes and sighed. "Because he's locked up."

Brian raised an eyebrow. "Really? Could he have called you from jail?"

She relaxed her elbow against the arm of the couch. "He doesn't have access. Besides, I know his voice."

Brian swallowed, willing himself to stay focused. "What is he in jail for?"

"Killing someone."

"If it isn't him, who do you think might be stalking you?"

"I don't know. Could be anyone."

"Are you worried about your safety?"

Her finger interlocked a strand of hair, as she seemed to consider that question. "I just want the feeling to go away."

Brian studied his legal pad. "Ms. Stephens, I think it might be a good idea if we talk about all of your past relationships."

She laughed. "We don't have that long."

"Then we'll schedule another appointment. But I think it's important."

"Why?"

He folded his hands and looked at her. "Because it's possible that one of the men from your past is still holding a grudge."

Krissy licked her lips, keeping her gaze locked on his. "Fine. I'll talk about them if you answer my one question."

"What's that?"

She leaned forward. "Are you married?"

"I think we need to stick to talking about you." He shifted in his chair.

Krissy slowly rose from the couch, dropped a hotel key card in his lap, and whispered. "I don't really care either way." She murmured the room number as she walked out the door.

4

Brian clicked off his light and locked up his office.

Danielle sat at the desk as he passed by. He smiled, but she didn't return it. Instead, she pursed her lips and turned away. That was odd. Maybe she had a bad day.

The elevator seemed stuck on some floor. He decided to take the stairs. Like a kid, he took two at a time. For some reason, he felt lighter this afternoon than he had in a while. He swung open the outside door and breathed deep.

Purple and orange rays painted the sky. *It is barely sunset. Way too early to go home.*

Just down the street, Brian pulled into the lot of a small brick building with black painted windows and a florescent sign that read, *Wally's Watering Hole.* He'd gone there once or twice before with an associate from work. He liked the quiet atmosphere and low-priced drinks.

He opened the rustic wooden door and glanced around the room. A single fluorescent light illuminated the tacky red décor. Rows of bottles lined the mirrored glass behind the bar, and half-a-dozen, mostly-empty tables were scattered about the room.

Brian walked past an old man in tattered clothes and a dark skinned woman with very little clothing, lots of makeup and big hair. He went to the end of the bar and straddled the stool.

"Can I get you something?" the bartender asked with a baritone voice.

Brian nodded to the ape-like man. "Whiskey and soda."

The bartender reached for a glass.

The under-dressed woman slipped off the stool and strolled Brian's way. "Hi sugar." She slid her arm next to his on the bar and batted her eyes. "You looking for a date?"

Brian raised his left hand and fingered his wedding ring so she could see it. "Sorry. I'm married."

The woman blew a bubble and shrugged. "Some of my best customers are married."

He angled away. "Not interested."

The woman put a red manicured fingernail to his chin. "That's too bad."

The bartender returned with his drink, and she sauntered away.

"Smart move," the bartender said. "She's dirty."

"She's what?" Brian lifted the glass to his lips.

"An undercover cop."

Brian peered at the woman over his glass. She stood in front of the bar mirror fluffing her hair. He gulped down the remainder of his drink and motioned for another. "I'm really not interested, anyway. I'm married."

"Good to hear." The bartender grabbed a bottle and squirted the whiskey into a small shot glass, tossed it into a bigger glass filled with soda, and then topped it off with a cherry. "I'm Walter, but everyone calls me Wally."

"Brian."

Wally stuck out his huge hand and encompassed Brian's in a shake. "If there's anything you need to get off your chest, I'm a good listener."

"Yeah?" Brian laughed and pulled the cherry from its stem with his teeth.

"Seriously. People tell me their problems all the time."

Brian held up his hand. "No, I believe you. It's just, I'm a psychologist."

Walter smiled. "So, you've probably said that a few times yourself."

Brian downed his drink and blinked to clear his watery eyes. "It's what I do." His voice cracked.

"I guess we have that in common," Wally said. "Only I didn't have to spend ten years in college to counsel. Two months in a technical school and I am everybody's therapist."

Brian reached for a basket of pretzels. "Yeah, I guess so."

"Would you like another drink?"

"Yeah. But just whiskey, no soda or ice."

Wally poured his drink, and then withdrew a rag under the counter. "So, what brings you here tonight?"

Brian didn't want to answer, but alcohol always loosened his tongue. When his inhibitions came down, he seemed to become someone else. *Maybe that's why I drink.* There was no love left for the man he'd become. He hated himself. "I'm avoiding the woman at home," Brian said.

"Ah. So, the marriage isn't as happy as you made Tracy believe."

"Tracy?"

Wally made a quick nod to the other end of the bar and smiled a keyboard grin. "The phony prostitute."

"Oh." Brian nodded.

Tracy glanced their way, and then swayed hip-to-hip out the door.

"No, my wife is indisposed. Or a better description, she's comatose. We haven't talked in months. Maybe years. I've lost track." Brian gestured for another drink. "Doesn't mean I don't love her, though. It's just hard to be around her."

Wally snorted and poured more amber liquid in Brian's glass. "Yeah, well, I wish I could get my ol' lady to shut up."

Brian chortled and the room swayed. "I think I'd better go." He downed the rest of his drink, pulled a few bills from his wallet and slapped them on the counter. "Thanks, Wally."

"Anytime."

Brian staggered toward the door.

"Hey man, you need a cab?" Wally asked.

"Nah, I've got it covered. Thanks." Brian pushed on the door. The damp night air nipped at his face. He stepped forward and the ground seemed to shift below his feet. He pulled his keys from his pocket and noticed Tracy watching him from a nearby streetlight. He popped his trunk and pulled out his cell phone.

Brian held up the phone so she could see it and dialed information. "San Diego. Cab company, please." Brian heard a few clicking noises and then the operator came on. "Yes, I need a cab sent to *Wally's Watering Hole* on Fifth and Palm. Thank you." Brian bent down to grab his briefcase from the trunk

A woman's voice spoke behind him. "Going somewhere?"

"Look, Ms. Tracy, I know you're a cop, and I've ordered a cab—" Brian turned and stopped.

Krissy Stephens.

"Hi." Brian cleared his throat.

Krissy raised an eyebrow. "Who's Ms. Tracy?"

"She's a prostitute, who's really a cop."

The corners of her mouth turned up. "Hmm. I see."

"Don't ask." He batted at the air. "So, what are you doing here?"

"I live over there in that condo." She pointed to a lone yellow door facing the street.

Brian glanced back at her. She looked more beautiful than before. Her smooth skin glowed in the amber streetlight. He knew he should send her away, but something—probably the many shots of alcohol in his system—kept him from dismissing her. His body swayed a bit.

She reached for his arm. "Do you need a ride?"

He looked down at her hand. "I have a cab coming."

"So you told Tracy." She smiled, and then slowly withdrew her hand. "How far do you live from here?"

Brian didn't answer.

"I understand. Client/therapist relationship." Krissy inched close enough for Brian to feel her warm breath on the side of his face. "What if I don't come back for therapy? Could we go out, then?"

Brian sighed. "I'm married."

"I figured that out. You've got that look," she said, pointing to his wedding ring.

A taxi pulled up to the curb and honked.

Brian allowed himself to meet her gaze. "Well, my ride's here."

"I guess so." She grazed his cheek with hers, and the slight hint of vanilla filled his nostrils. "I made an appointment for next Thursday. I'll see you then."

Brian slammed the trunk of his car and stumbled to the yellow car.

Tracy had vanished from her spot.

Brian stepped inside the cab and glanced back to where Krissy stood.

"401 St. Augustine in Scripps Ranch," he said as he shut the door. They pulled away and Brian laid his head against the seat. His emotions struggled to find reason. His head pounded. All reality was submerged in whiskey.

∂∽⟨∽

Ray pushed open the front door with his foot and awkwardly maneuvered two grocery sacks and a twelve-pack of soda onto the kitchen counter. The air in the room felt thick and warm. He shut the front door to his apartment, and then crossed to the balcony window. He slid it open and inhaled deep.

The sounds of cars rushed by below and lights lined the city. Why he ever wanted to live Downtown was a mystery.

His mother tried to talk him into getting a condo by the golf course. She said it would be a great excuse to relax. But he knew better. She wanted a reason to move back in with her boy.

He was lonely. Maybe it was time to give in.

But then images of her nagging him returned. He shook his head and pulled out a box of pre-made nugget strips.

The doorbell rang.

He dropped the box back in the bag and started for the door. "Who is it?"

"Me," came a familiar woman's voice. "We need to talk."

5

Brian quietly opened the door to his home. The house was dark, except for the stove light in the kitchen. He dropped his keys and wallet on the table by the door and felt for the lamp. All was quiet. He knew Rhonda would be asleep, but his guilt for coming home drunk made him pause. He'd be happier if she'd just wake up and react to his ghastly behavior. Maybe if she'd slap his face raw, then he would feel alive again. A heated argument would be welcome to this emotional famine any day.

Brian opened the bedroom door and pulled off his shoes. The cadence of his wife's breathing filled the air. He placed his shoes in the closet and undressed down to boxers. He stretched out next to Rhonda. The movement of the bed synchronized with the rhythm of her breathing. In and out. In and out.

For a moment, her breathing stopped. He turned to face her, and she resumed. In. Out. In. Out. He lay back, and stared at the ceiling. The more she breathed, the more he gasped for air. Her every breath seemed to suck the air from his chest. In. Out. His heart accelerated. The pulse in his neck quickened. He shot up, hyperventilating.

I'm having a heart attack. He grabbed at his chest. *No, just an anxiety attack. Remain calm.* But the words in his head did little to soothe him. He snatched his robe from the door and rushed into the kitchen.

Flinging on the faucet, he plunged his face into the running water. "What is wrong with me?" he said aloud.

"I can answer that," a voice said from behind him.

Brian spun around, dripping wet. His daughter sat on a stool at the breakfast counter, smiling ear to ear.

"Lara?" Hiding behind the black terrycloth robe in his hand, he seized a paper towel to wipe his face. "How long have you been there?"

"Long enough."

He pulled on the robe and tied the sash. "You startled me."

"Then we're even." She smiled. "Are you OK?"

"I'm just a little shaken, that's all." He tossed the towel in the trash under the sink.

"How come?"

Brian opened the refrigerator, grabbed a bottle of water, and sat on the stool next to her. "I think your Mom's condition is starting to wear on me."

"Have you talked to her yet?"

"Yes, and she doesn't talk back. Have you noticed that she's a zombie?"

Lara pursed her lips into a pout. It was how he remembered her as a small girl. "Maybe she's a zombie because you see her that way."

"What?"

She took a sip from his water bottle. "She seems fine to me, but you think she's crazy."

"Really? If she's so fine, tell me the last time she talked to you?"

Lara thought about that for a second. "I guess, before the accident."

"Precisely." He took back his water and took a drink. "That was a long time ago. Don't you think that's a little odd?"

"No."

"How can you say that? She's your mother. A mother who refuses to take care of you. The doctors say she's fine and she could talk if she wanted to. She chooses to sleep all the time."

Lara shook her head. "You know, Dad, for a shrink, you sure don't have many answers."

Brian stared at her. "And for someone your age, you're a bit of a smart aleck."

"Hey, it's in the genes."

He smiled and squeezed her around the shoulders. "Yeah, that's probably true."

They both laughed.

"Well, I'm going to bed. See you in the morning, Daddy." She kissed his cheek, stood up and walked down the hall.

Brian called after her. "You didn't tell me why you don't think mom's behavior is odd."

"Oh, Daddy, you're not ready." And she disappeared up the stairs.

⊱⊰

Danielle sat up at the sound of her phone ringing and croaked into the phone, "Hello?"

"Hi."

She didn't recognize the male voice. The clock read one in the morning. "Who is this?"

"Brian Manifold."

Adrenaline coursed through her body. Everything froze. What did she do? Reason said to hang up. Why was he calling her?

"Are you still there?" he asked.

"Yeah, um, why are you calling me? It's one in the morning."

He let out a long chuckle. "I just needed to talk to someone. You're someone I can talk to, right?"

"No, not really."

He blew through his lips. "Yeah, I noticed you were a little cold today. Who put the burr under your saddle?"

The man was clearly drunk. Anger rose up her back. "Dr. Manifold…"

"Brian, please."

"Doctor, you're married. The only thing you should be doing right now is climbing in bed with your wife and going to sleep."

A long silence held the line.

She moved to hang up—

"I can't. But thank you."

The line buzzed in her ear. What should she make of that? Should she tell someone? Would he get in trouble? No. She needed to just let him be. Obviously, he'd had a bit too much to drink. Maybe he'd sleep it off and totally forget he'd ever called her.

❧❦

Brian sat on the cream-colored couch with the phone in his hand afraid to attempt sleep again. The conversation with Lara kept replaying in his mind. He'd called Danielle to block it out, but she didn't really want to talk to him.

How could a mother ignore her child? It didn't make sense. Especially if anyone knew the Rhonda he'd married. She was a strong woman, with a heart of gold. Ray was right. She used to be Brian's world.

Thoughts of the way things used to be filtered through his mind. Every night she made him a fantastic meal, usually from scratch. Her beef stroganoff was his favorite. Then she'd make hot soda with lemon, and they'd curl up in front of the fireplace and talk about their days.

His heart ached. How he missed her. The woman who slept in his bed was not his wife. The snoring zombie was an imposter. A thief who had stolen his heart and murdered his love.

The light reflected off the glass in his hand. He focused on the water for a moment until his vision blurred. He felt like crying. Instead, he finished off his water and sighed. He really wanted a drink with kick, but he knew better than to bring alcohol into the house. He could remember the many threats his wife had made about him drinking. And even though he knew she'd probably never know, he felt like he'd betray her if he did.

Maybe he'd sleep out here tonight. Brian grabbed a decorative pillow from the end of the couch and stretched out. He closed his eyes, but couldn't relax. His mind whirled unsettled, his body restless. He rolled onto his side in an attempt to get comfortable, but his six-foot-three frame hung over both ends of the lumpy sofa.

"Useless," he said aloud. He turned over and stared at the blank TV screen. He needed to sleep, but he wasn't about to go back into his bedroom. He turned over a few more times, before he decided to forgo any slumber. He glanced around the room as if the furniture had answers to his insomnia. His high-back chair sat empty to his left. A walled bookshelf stood to his right.

The décor was simple. Black and white photos of Rhonda and him framed the room, and a wedding picture sat over the fireplace to the right of the TV in front of him. Before the accident, his wife was stunning.

Stop! He ran a hand over his face and sat up. It was stupid to dwell on better days. Where was the remote? He switched on the television and channel surfed through the stations.

Sports, cheesy old movies, and sitcom reruns. Nothing worth watching. He snapped it off, flipped on his back, and stared at the vaulted ceiling. He figured he'd stay awake all night, but alone with his thoughts, he soon drifted into a deep sleep.

6

Ray made his way down the corridor toward the cafeteria, head down, secretly chastising himself for agreeing to eat lunch with Danielle Tyler. Not his smartest move. Gossip and innuendo would certainly follow. People would assume the worst, as they always did. He cringed at the thought. No way was he this comfortable with the idea. So why did he keep walking? After all, he'd had enough controversy over the past few months. Was he really ready for another?

No he wasn't. He stopped a few feet from the cafeteria door and shook his head. This was stupid. He needed to remember why he accepted this "date" in the first place. It wasn't for the reasons most would think. True, she was a knock-out blonde with the most amazing blue eyes, but this lunch had purpose—to talk about his good friend, Brian. Was there any truth to the rumors that his married colleague had gone out with Danielle?

Ray continued forward and entered the room.

The pretty blonde smiled at him with her apple-red lips. Everyone kept their distance because of the office buzz that surrounded her. But what if the gossip about Danielle and Brian wasn't true?

Would Ray feel free to date her? He squeezed his eyes closed and faced the refrigerated display case. *Date her?* He didn't date anyone. This entire thing made him super nervous. Not that she'd know that.

Ray had perfected the façade of confidence. Most people thought he was a ladies' man, but they were wrong.

He reached for plastic bowl filled with melon balls and sighed. He wasn't ready.

క≫≪ఌ

Danielle toyed with the plastic wrap on her salad, waiting for Ray to join her.

His shoulders were erect, making him appear confident, assured of who he was.

If only she could be that way. Maybe some of the ideas people had about her would go away. She wasn't a blonde bimbo. She graduated top of her class in college, ministered in her church, and hadn't had a real date in over three years. Just because she flirted with Brian once or twice, before she knew his marital status, everyone assumed terrible things—things that she would *never* do. It amazed her how one mistake—an innocent one at that—affected her so fast. She winced at the thought.

Ray joined her, sitting in the booth across from her. He tore a wrapper from his straw, crumbled it into a ball and tossed it aside. "You going to eat?" he asked, eyeing her sealed food.

She grinned. "Yeah, I was just being polite, waiting for you."

"Well, thank you, but you didn't have to wait." He winked, and stuffed his straw into the lid of his cup. "Dig in, please."

She unwrapped the cellophane from the top of her California salad and then smothered it in blue cheese dressing. The grilled chicken and avocado looked great. Unfortunately, she wasn't a bit hungry with Ray less than five feet away.

"How long have you worked here, Ms. Tyler?"

"Danielle, please." She shook a packet of sweetener and dumped it in her iced tea. "About six months."

He cleared his throat and met her stare. "I need to ask you something a tad embarrassing. I hope you won't be offended."

Oh no, he found out I like him. This can't be good. She swallowed and nodded. "Go ahead."

"It would be helpful for me if you're honest, but I'll respect your privacy."

"OK," she said gnawing nervously on a carrot.

"How well do you know Dr. Manifold?"

Danielle peered out the window, now afraid of where this conversation might end. "I see him every day. I wouldn't say we're friends, but I'm well aware of his presence."

"Don't take this the wrong way, but I have to know if" — He pursed his lips for a moment. "Did you and he ever" —

"Did we ever get together?" she finished for him.

Ray nodded, but his gaze remained focused on his plate.

"No," she said. "We flirted a little. But when I found out he was a married man, well, despite what people might think around here, I'm not that type of woman."

"I see." Ray took a sip of his soda. "The man I knew would never have flirted with you. He loved his wife. I'm disturbed by what's happening to him."

"I understand. I think he's a nice man, Dr. Jensen."

"Have you noticed anything else going on with

him?"

The other day flooded her memory. She bit her lip, considering if she should tell.

"What?"

"Yeah, I suppose I did, once." Danielle glanced around the room and lowered her voice. "He called me at home, drunk, around one in the morning."

"At home?"

"Yeah. It was pretty odd. I didn't even know he knew my number."

"Did you tell anyone this before now?"

She shook her head. "I was afraid to. Like I said, he's a nice guy. I really hate to get him in trouble."

"I think he's doing a nice enough job of that himself." Ray frowned. "Thanks, Ms. Tyler. You've been real helpful." He clutched his tray and rose to go. "I'll let you enjoy your lunch now."

He couldn't leave.

Danielle looked him in the eye. "You didn't finish your food."

"I wasn't really hungry. I just needed a chance to talk to you." He scooted his chair out. "Thanks for your time."

"Sure."

He grinned, a gorgeous smile that lit up his face and her heart. "I'll be seeing you around. Be sure to take a break now and then."

"I will," she said, staring at him like a schoolgirl with an enormous crush.

"Bye."

He waved and sauntered down the hall.

Danielle couldn't stop smiling, nor could she really eat. Though the subject matter of their meal wasn't all that enjoyable, the *idea* of it was. He was such a great guy. It hurt her feelings that the only reason he lunched with her was for information. But that information was important for them. Now that she'd put the rumors to rest in his mind, maybe, just maybe, he'd ask her out for a real date someday. The subtle looks he sent her way gave her hope. Of course, his mind was obviously preoccupied with all things Dr. Manifold.

❧❦

Brian was grateful to be back at work. The majority of his patients were troubled teens on their way to Juvenile Hall, but he loved his young patients. He'd chosen the subject of peer rejection for his dissertation, primarily because a lot of his clients blamed inferiority for their destructive social situations. Some turned to drugs or gang activity. Others sought suicidal or homicidal solutions to make them feel alive—if only for the moment.

The door opened to his office and a young man entered, dressed in layers of black, spiked hair, and covered in piercings.

Jake. His new patient's former address was Juvenile Hall, but now he lived in a halfway house awaiting trial.

Brian gave himself a mental pat on the back for taking on such a difficult patient. "So, Jake, tell me why you were arrested?" Brian settled back into his leather chair and studied the boy.

"Man, I was framed." The pale youth nudged his black combat boot against the side of the coffee table and smiled as a crystal figurine dropped onto the floor.

Brian picked up the figurine and met his stare.

"You know, you aren't the first person to say that to me."

"I'm sure." He glanced around the room, apparently trying to avoid Brian's stare.

Brian repositioned himself to address his patient better. "As a matter of fact, it is the most common phrase uttered in this office."

"Yeah?" The young man slumped back and stared at the ceiling.

Brian studied the chart in his lap. *This isn't working.* He had to change tactics. "So, what I'm to understand is, you didn't do it?"

"Yeah, man, that's what I said." Jake stood and paced the room.

"Suppose you tell me why the police think you murdered someone?"

Jake didn't look up from his pacing. "I was at the wrong place—"

"At the wrong time."

"Now you get it, Doc. I didn't do it."

"Do you want to talk about it?"

"Nah."

Brian swallowed and worked to keep his tone low and his voice impassive. "What do you propose we do with our time, then?"

"Beats me." Jake shrugged. "I didn't ask to be here."

Brian crossed to where Jake stood, grabbed a fairly new black book from the bookshelf and held it out.

Jake recoiled as if the book was on fire. "What's that for?"

"It's a Bible."

"I know it's a Bible, man." He glared at Brian. "I want to know why you're trying to give it to me. I think it's pretty clear that I'm not some religious freak."

Brian smiled. "It's simple. You can do one of two things with our time. You can sit down and talk to me about what really happened, or you can read this. My wife calls this book 'truth,' and since that is what I need from you, I think you could use some of it yourself." Brian turned and walked back to his seat.

"You're weird."

Brian shrugged and grabbed his cup of coffee. "I've been called worse."

Jake puckered his lips and stared at the Bible. Slowly, he glanced from the book to Brian. "Fine." The boy snatched the book, plopped on the couch, flung his boots onto the armrest, and cracked it open.

In all the years Brian had pulled that trick, Jake was the first person to take him up on it. *And the least likely.* Brian sat in amazement as the ghostly-pale adolescent read the world's most controversial book.

Brian was not a Christian man by any means, but Rhonda was a devout believer and had given him the Bible as a birthday gift a few years ago.

He'd opened it a few times to read about the life of Jesus. He found the story of Jesus' rejection intriguing, especially in light of Brian's theories on peer rejection. Puzzling how a noble man like Jesus could have the sympathetic ear of the people one day and their insistent call for death the next.

Brian sighed and returned to his desk. What else to do, but let Jake read the Bible for the rest of the hour? It couldn't hurt.

When the timer went off, Jake tossed the Bible on the couch and stretched. "I guess I'll see you next week. Thanks for the session, Doc."

Brian glanced at his watch and nodded.

The young man waved over his shoulder and ambled out the door.

Brian placed the Bible back on the shelf. Someone moved behind him. He spun around.

"Hey," Ray said, entering Brian's office. "I hear your research is finally published. That's great. I look forward to having a signed copy."

Brian frowned. *Good day over.* "What do you want, Ray? I have an appointment in a few minutes, and I still need to read her chart."

"Why are you never excited to see me anymore?" Ray grabbed a piece of candy from the coffee table and popped it in his mouth.

"Because...every time you visit *this* floor, something's wrong." Brian walked behind his desk.

"That hurts."

Brian rolled his eyes, and began writing in a file in hopes that Ray would take the hint and leave. When he didn't, Brian asked, "Do you deny it?"

"Deny what?"

Brian stopped writing and looked up. "Why are you here, Ray?"

"OK, you caught me." He smirked and shut the door. "We need to talk."

Ray sat.

Brian did not.

"Brian," Ray said, his tone flat and taut. "You know I care about you, so I hate to be the bad guy."

Brian snorted. *Yeah, right.* He noticed the tightness in Ray's jaw. *Here we go.*

"Things aren't going well for you."

"What isn't going well? My calendar is full. I'm about to be published. Life is great!" Brian offered the cheesiest smile he could muster.

"Brian, you know this hospital isn't a private practice. You work for *them*. They sign your check; you're under their rules. That means you need to be at work at nine o'clock every morning and you need to stay until six. You show respect and you maintain a certain level of dignity." Ray's voice rose, but Brian could tell he was holding back. "You're failing on all counts."

"I'm not sure what you're talking about. So, I've been late a few times."

"Come on, Brian. When was the last time you came to a mandatory council meeting?"

Brian pretended to think about that. "Hmm? It's been a while... "

"Try months. And how many times have you been late in the last few weeks?"

"Listen, things are hard at home right now. I've been dealing with stuff that sometimes makes it hard to get here on time." It was sort of the truth. "I'll try to do better."

"I completely understand. What happened to you would shake any man." Ray leaned forward. "That's why I really think you need to take some time off and—"

"No! I told you before, I need to work."

Ray stared at him a moment before responding. "Fine. But you need to know that I won't be able to protect you much longer. It'll soon be out of my hands. If you keep messing up, the hospital will recommend that you go to the licensing board for evaluation."

"What?" Brian stood with tightened fists positioned on his desk. "That's ridiculous! I thought you said you were my friend."

"I *am* your friend, Brian." Ray sighed. "That's why I'm here. To assist you. To warn you. Whatever it takes to help you succeed."

"No," Brian said through clenched teeth, "you're here to tell me to get my act together because I am starting to make *you* look bad."

Ray shook his head. "Did I, or did I not, come down here yesterday and tell you to be at the meeting."

"Yeah...so?"

"I did that out of friendship. I knew that Dr. Jai would be in attendance and would be looking for you...and when the hospital VP looks for someone, he'd better find them." Ray stepped forward and placed his hand on the edge of Brian's desk. "I've risked my own position to defend you, and you're right; your negligence is starting to reflect on me." Ray sighed. "But, I do care. I don't want you to fail. I have your best interest in mind. You have to believe that."

Sure I do. "Look, I don't need your help. I haven't done anything wrong."

"How can you say that?" Ray shook his head. "Haven't you been listening to anything I've said?"

"Look, my next client will be here any moment. I really have to get prepared."

Ray stared at Brian's desk, and then backed toward the door. "I'll go for now. But you need to know that I'm truly worried about you. If you don't get help soon, I'll be forced to disclose what I know about your job performance."

Brian narrowed his eyes. "And you'll just be doing your job, right?"

"Yes, that's right."

Brian gave Ray a sardonic grin, and for an

awkward moment, both men glared at each other.

"Very well. I'll talk to you later." Ray turned and left without another word.

Brian sighed with relief. He looked at his calendar and saw that he had a full schedule after lunch. *I can't go home, and yet, I don't feel like working, either.* He opened the drawer to the right of his desk, removed a small leather flask, and glanced at the door before unscrewing the cap. He placed the mouthpiece on his lips and shot his head back. The liquid burned his throat. Squinting against the power of the drink, Brian replaced the cap on the bottle.

Rhonda hated that he drank.

It's all those church goodie-goodies. Whatever her reason, he tried to keep his habit to himself. *Of course, it isn't really a habit.* He just used the occasional nip to calm his nerves. Unfortunately, his nerves were more raw than usual lately. He shrugged it off. *She's too preoccupied with sleeping to notice.*

His phone buzzed. He flicked the intercom button. "Yes?"

"Ms. Robinson is here to see you."

"Send her in." He sighed loudly. Back to work.

7

Danielle stared at the clock wondering where Ray was this morning. A dozen times, she tried to call him, ask him out. But instead, she was a big chicken staring at the minute hand creeping by. *I wonder what he did last night. Is he dating anyone?*

"Are you working today?" Brian asked.

Danielle glanced up, startled. "Um, yeah. Guess I just drifted off for a moment. Did you need something Dr. Manifold?"

"Brian, please." He winked.

She dropped her gaze, ashamed that she'd just been too friendly. How did she shoo him away without being rude? *Maybe I need to be rude.* "Listen, Dr. Manifold, this is hard to say..." She took a deep breath. "Look, I know you're married."

His smile disappeared.

"I think you're a nice man and all, but under the circumstances, I think we need to be nothing more than professional colleagues."

"And what? You thought we were something else?" He crossed his arms, narrowed his eyes. "I would expect more from you, Ms. Tyler."

"Yes, sir. Of course, sir." Her stomach twisted in pain. This man had the ability to have her fired. Though his flirting was real, it would be her word against his. And he would win. "May I help you with something?"

He cleared his throat. "I was wondering if you've seen Dr. Jensen."

"No." Her pulse quickened at the thought of her real interest. "He's usually here by now."

"Yes, well, have a good day," He said under his breath as he turned, but loud enough that she could hear. "Now I know I will."

The elevator opened and Ray stepped out.

Danielle sat upright, hoping she looked OK. Truthfully, she had been taking a bit longer to get ready lately. She imagined her Uncle Ison saying, "To catch a fish, you need some bait."

Ray walked to the counter and smiled. "Good morning."

"Hi," she said nervously. "Did you come down here to see Dr. Manifold?"

"No. Why?"

"He was just looking for you."

His eyebrow rose. "Really?"

She didn't mention Brian's last comment. "Yeah. He didn't say what he wanted."

"OK, thanks." Ray nodded, and started to walk away.

"Dr. Jensen?"

He faced her again. "Yes?"

"If he wasn't the reason you came down here, what was?"

"I'll share that with you later." He winked and continued to Brian's office.

☙◦❧

Ray sat in his own high-backed brown leather chair and sighed. His encounter with Brian hadn't gone so well. Not that he hadn't known that would be the case. *I hate this. It's hard to believe we were best friends once. Ten years of college filled with tough classes, campus politics, and even falling for the same girl our first year.* Ray smiled at the memory. Of course, Ray never had the guts to ask her out, so Brian won the girl.

Ray's gaze drifted to the harbor outside the window; his smile slid away. *How did it get to this?* The Brian he knew was gone and unreachable. *I know it's been hard since the accident, but...* Another sigh escaped. *The pressure is squashing him, and there is nothing I can do to help him.*

He reached into his drawer and withdrew a bag of soy crisp cakes. Staring at the dried cracker, he grimaced. He hated them, but after finding out he was prone to diabetes, his doctor insisted he cut back on regular snacks.

He bit into the cracker and sighed. *I feel OK.* But the doctors knew differently. Brian was the same. *He says he feels fine, but inside his soul is screaming. Lord, please help Brian. He needs You, and only You can get him through this.*

The phone rang.

He answered and winced. "Mother."

"Why haven't you called me?"

"I meant to, but things are a little crazy here at the office." He tossed his half-eaten cracker into the garbage and sighed. "What do you need? I'm a bit busy."

"Does a mother need something to call her boy?"

"Yes, usually you do."

He pictured her corpulent body wedged tightly in her sunflower-yellow rocking chair, watching DVDs.

"OK, you caught me. There's this girl at my Bible

study on Wednesdays…"

He thrust his hand out. "OK, stop right there, Mother!"

"You don't even know what I am going to say. "

"Yes, I do." He sighed. "You're hoping to set me up, am I right?"

"She's a lovely girl. She's in medicine like you. Works at a veterinary hospital out in El Cajon."

"I don't care."

"Oh, now, come on. You have to meet her."

He chuckled, despite the fury rising in his throat. "No, Mom, I don't."

"And why not?"

"Because the last time I went along with this, the woman had a mustache and a bug collection." His skin still crawled at her horrible hyena laugh.

"I want grandchildren in this lifetime." She huffed. "Isn't there anyone you could date? You're not a bad looking man. I don't understand why you've had such trouble finding a wife."

"I have a lot of work to do, Mom."

"I'm just saying."

He closed his eyes and breathed deep. "I love you, but we're not going to talk about this. I need to go."

"She really is cute."

"Good bye." He hung up and laid his head on his desk. Between his best friend and his mother, he was going to lose his mind.

❧

Sylvia—a New York youth of Italian decent—sat across from Brian smacking her gum.

Pop!

It had been less than thirty minutes and Brian tried to remain calm. *I don't know how much more of this I can take. She looks like a cow chewing a cud.* He couldn't help but focus on her mouth. *Chew, chew, pop!* Her words echoed in his head; her teeth masticated her cud of gum.

"So, you see, doctor," Sylvia said, "I'm not sure why Ronnie doesn't want me anymore. *Pop!*

Brian rubbed his temples. *I've got a few ideas*, he thought, but said, "Well, Sylvia, I think we'll finish up next week."

Sylvia looked at her watch. "But it's only been a half hour." *Pop!*

Brian cringed. "Yes, but I've got an incredible migraine, and I don't know how much help I can be to you right now." Brian stood and motioned for her to do the same.

"I'm sorry, Dr. Manifold. Have you taken anything to help with the headache? My Aunt Lola always used to say that two aspirins and caffeine soda is just the thing to knock it right out." *Pop!*

Brian forced a grin. "That's excellent advice. I'm sure I'll be fine after I try that." *And you leaving wouldn't hurt, either.*

"Well, OK." Sylvia pulled at her tight-fitting leather skirt, grabbed her purse, and sauntered to the door. "Should I make another appointment for later this week?"

"I'm booked for the rest of this week, but talk to Sheila on your way out. She'll be able to set something up for you."

"Thank you, doctor."

Brian closed the door behind her and collapsed in his desk chair. Brian heard another of Sylvia's fractured bubbles echo down the hallway. He buzzed Sheila.

"Yes, sir?"

"From now on, please make sure that all my patients spit out their gum before entering my office, understood?"

"Sir?"

"Please, Sheila. Absolutely no more gum chewing is allowed during counseling sessions. It's distracting. Understood?"

"Yes, sir."

"Thank you."

"Sir?"

"Yes, Sheila?"

"Your next appointment is here."

Brian groaned. "Send him in."

8

Two women stood across the lobby staring at Danielle, whispering. A usual occurrence these days. Thank goodness, she had a few friends in the lion's den.

"Don't let them get to you," Ray said.

Danielle glanced up and smiled. "Good morning, Dr. Jensen. Was I that obvious?"

He turned to look at the gossiping pair and nodded. "People are dumb. The Bible even says as much."

"Really?" She laughed, and then grew serious. "Yeah, well, it changes everything."

His forehead creased. "Like what?"

Could she say it? Actually spill what she was thinking? Weeks of mooning over this man, she needed the courage. "Like you, for instance."

"Me?"

She licked her lips, struggling with a way to continue. "Yeah, you."

Resting his elbows on the counter, he leaned toward her. "Explain, please."

Big breath in. "Well, when you heard the rumor, it affected your opinion of me. I'm guessing that you will probably never ask me out, because you assume the rumors are true, even though I told you they weren't."

He sat back up, a slight grin tugging at his lip. "You think I haven't asked you out because of the rumors?"

So stupid. Why did I say that? "Um, or there could be a million other reasons, I'm sure."

"My dear, that has nothing to do with it."

Her expression fell. *How could I be this ridiculous?* Her skin warmed. She probably looked like an embarrassed tomato. If only there was an "undo" button on life.

"No, wait." He held up his hands and laughed. "That sounded bad."

"A little. Yes."

"The truth is I'm kind of shy. I haven't dated in a really long time."

"How long?" she heard herself say.

His gaze dropped down, as if studying his hands. "I think that answer would tarnish your opinion of me forever."

"Then I won't feel alone. Shoot."

He cleared his throat, and then glanced over both shoulders to make sure no one was listening. "Since my freshman year in college."

The shock of his confession had to show on her face. She knew her eyes were wide.

"Anyway—" He slapped the counter and added a cheesy grin. "So, yeah. There it is."

"OK, now I'm curious. Why not? I mean...you're a good looking man." A shy smile escaped her lips.

"I'm refusing to answer this time." He stepped back as if to go, but then added, "But if I did date, you'd be my first pick."

Her heart did a somersault into her stomach. An internal warning chided her to maintain some sort of control, but she couldn't wipe the grin from her face. "And if you ever feel ready to ask, I'll say yes."

Their gazes locked, and a surge of energy passed between them, she was sure of it.

Merle stepped out her office with a stack of files. "Danielle, could you stop by the records office? Oh, hello, Dr. Jensen. Did you need something?"

He glanced over Danielle's shoulder, and the spell was broken. "No, thank you. Your assistant, Ms. Tyler, has been very helpful."

Danielle pinched her lips together to avoid laughing. "Glad to be of service."

"We'll talk again."

"I look forward to it." She gave a mischievous grin. "You know, when you're ready."

He winked and walked down the hall.

Oh my. Danielle's heart fluttered at top speed.

"Danielle?"

She spun to Merle in a daze. "I'm sorry. What did you need for me to do?"

∾∾

Brian turned off the green banker's lamp that sat on his desk. A soft amber glow shadowed his office through the cracks in the shade. He crossed to the window and pulled back the blinds. The San Diego skyline glistened like illuminated diamonds in the night. Brian sipped from the drink in his hand and sighed. He dreaded going home. The woman who lay in his bed constantly reminded him how wrong his life was at the moment. He walked back to his seat and refilled his glass.

Someone knocked on the door. "Come in."

An older Hispanic man dressed in tan overalls stuck his head in the door. "Excuse me, Dr. Manifold.

Would you mind if I dumped your garbage?"

Pete. Brian pushed a pencil holder in front of his glass and motioned for the custodian to enter.

"I would have waited for you to leave, but I'm trying to get to my son's play tonight."

Brian forced a smile.

"He's playing Horatio in *Hamlet*. You ever see it?" Pete dumped the trash in a large metal bin on wheels.

Brian cleared his throat. "No, I can't say that I have."

"Yeah." Pete nodded as if Brian had said something profound. "Hard to understand that guy, but he's famous."

Brian blinked. "That guy?"

"Shakespeare."

"Right." Brian eyed the drink, wanting desperately to finish it.

"Yeah. My son's a regular thespian. Loves that stuff." Instead of moving to the door, he rattled on some more. "I wanted him to play football, but my wife insisted he follow his gifting. My favorite play was that one with the shy girl who had all those glass animals. Do you know which one I mean?"

Brian knew, but he shook his head. *Why won't he just leave?*

"Oh, what was it called?" The custodian looked at the ceiling and snapped his fingers a few times. "Oh, I hate that. Don't you just hate that?"

No, I hate when people like you don't just do your job and get out of my office, so I can finish my drink in peace. "Yes, of course." Brian deliberately looked at his watch.

It worked. "Oh, I'm sorry. I know I talk a lot. Besides, I don't want to miss the rise." He smiled.

"That's stage talk for the beginning of the show."

Brian nodded, but didn't return the smile.

Pete backed his cart out, and then snapped his fingers. "*The Glass Menagerie.* That's right. The play I was talking about. Have you seen it?"

Brian shook his head.

"You really should. I loved it."

"I'll be sure to do that," Brian said dryly.

The man nodded. "Good night, Dr. Manifold."

"Good night." Brian stared at the closed door, and then grabbed his glass. He downed the remainder of the caramel-colored liquid and breathed deeply. *Time to get out of here.* He set down the glass, walked to the door, and turned the knob. Something stopped him. *What was that?* He turned around slowly and scanned the office.

Empty.

A shadow reflected from the drawn blinds. His heart raced. *It's probably just the alcohol in my system. Maybe I'm seeing things.* He grabbed an umbrella by the door and stepped back into the room.

"Hello? Danielle? Ray? Anybody there?"

Silence.

"Can we talk? I promise I won't turn you in. I just want to talk to you."

Brian stepped to the desk and flipped the light back on. He turned around.

Jake stood less than an inch behind him, sopping wet.

Brian's heart shot into his stomach. He jerked backward and knocked the phone off his desk. "Jake?" He tried to regain his composure and reached for the phone. "My goodness, what are you doing here? It is after 8:00 PM. The office closed hours ago."

"We need to talk."

"Why don't we book an appointment for tomorrow?" Brian grabbed his calendar and pen. "I need to get home and you shouldn't be here."

"Tomorrow may be too late. We need to talk now."

Jake's face seemed whiter than usual. His eyes were red, hollow, moist with tears.

Brian perceived the urgency in the young man's face. He wasn't sure how to respond. If he sent Jake away and something bad happened, Brian would be held responsible.

Of course, there were certain protocols, rules, which were clearly set up between client and therapist for a good reason. This was unmistakably a breach of those guidelines.

"Jake, how'd you get in here?"

"I don't care. We have to talk." Jake stood defiant.

"Sure, but you need to know that this isn't the way things are done. You understand that, don't you?"

"Yeah, I get it. Now, can we talk?"

Brian grabbed a few tissues for him, and then motioned for Jake to sit. "OK, Jake," Brian grabbed a notepad from the desk and sat. "What's going on?"

Jake sheltered his pallid face between his spindly fingers and sobbed.

"It'll be all right, son." Brian said, soothing. He reached for the tissue box and set it down next to the boy's knee. "Will you tell me what's bothering you? I promise you'll feel much better once you get it out. Trust me, everyone always does."

Jake wiped his nose with the arm of his coat. "I think I'm ready to confess."

"What do you need to confess?" Brian handed him

another tissue.

Jake blew his nose, buried his face in his hands and started to cry again. Brian moved to the couch and patted the broken teenager on the shoulder. "This is good. Just let it out. You can't heal until you get rid of the mental poison in your mind."

Jake sniffed. "Poison?"

"It's a metaphor. I just meant in order to get well you have to be honest about the things that hurt you, and then let them go."

"How do I do that?"

"In this case you talk about the things that cause you pain."

Jake roughly wiped his eyes with his palms. "I don't know, Doc. I'm kind of scared."

"Well, of course you are. That's perfectly natural." Brian moved back to his chair. "Whenever you hold something in for any length of time it is hard to let it go. I think we become dependent on those things that hurt us."

Jake didn't answer. He just stared down at his hands, as if he was thinking.

Brian brought his folded hands to his chin and asked, "So, Jake, what would you like to tell me?"

"I didn't kill her exactly like you think."

"Kill who, Jake? Who did you kill?"

Jake shook his head. "Nope. Not going to tell you that," Jake smirked. "Nice try, though."

"Fine, don't tell me her name. Just tell me the story."

"It's been a while now, but I still remember it clearly. I was at this party in the valley and everybody was having a good time. People were toasting to some good news. Others danced and drank too much.

Looking around the party, it was obvious that nobody could have known what would happen next." Jake wiped at his eyes again. "Maybe if I had known I wouldn't have gone. And then, I wouldn't be here today. Who knows?" Jake sniffed.

"What happened at the party, Jake?"

Jake jumped up and started to pace. "It was a great night."

"I understand, son. Things happened that you probably didn't want to happen. Am I right?"

The young man stopped and faced Brian. Tears covered his face. "Yeah, nothing went right."

"Tell me about it," Brian said.

Jake let out a deep sigh. "I was so happy, and then everything went wrong."

"Tell me what happened, Jake? What went wrong?"

Jake stared intently for a moment, and then sat back in the chair. "I pushed someone by accident and she died."

"Pushed who?"

Jake stood and stepped to the window. "Why do you suppose we're here?"

"Pushed who, Jake?"

"I told you. I'm not going to answer that." Jake peeked through the blinds. "People who know me, I mean, who *really* know me, like me. Most other people judge me by what they see."

"And who are you?"

"I'm nobody," Jake said.

Brian crossed to where the young man stood. "I don't believe that. I think you just have to find how your piece fits in the world's puzzle." He patted the young man's back and added, "But first you have to be honest."

"Yeah, right!" Jake slapped the glass hard enough to make Brian jump. "Be honest. Now there's something that everyone seems to be good at." Jake faced Brian with piercing eyes. "No one is honest, Doc. No one."

Brian's stomach turned. Something in the way Jake said, "No one" made him feel uneasy. Like "no one" was actually another name for *Brian*. He swallowed. "Why do you feel that way?"

"Because everyone I know lives in a make believe world. They dress one way, but act another. Hypocrites!" Jake looked Brian over. "You put that suit on each day, and I bet you think it makes you a man. But I say you're a big fraud. I guarantee if you put on a pair of shorts and a T-shirt you'd be more yourself. Am I right?"

Brian ignored his question. "Why do you wear all black?"

Jake glanced down at his trench coat, and then to his city-camouflage pants and ripped t-shirt. "Because it's me. I don't want to fit into some mold."

"Ah, but you do."

"Oh, sure. I'd like to see you come to work dressed like this. I'm sure your boss would love that."

Brian sat back in his chair. "That mold you're wearing is found in every mall in San Diego. I see tons of kids just like you running around with purple hair and combat boots, spouting through their pierced lips that they're somehow unique. Ironically, they're all still mimicking someone else's style."

Jake jumped to his feet, his face red, his fist clenched. "I knew it! You're just like the rest, Doc. You're judging me by the way I look."

"I haven't judged you, Jake. I'm simply telling you what I see."

Jake stepped forward and pressed into Brian's chair. "And what do you see, doc?"

Brian's eye twitched and he labored to keep a stoic face. "A young man crying out for help."

Jake pushed back and laughed again. "No. I think it's you who needs help, doc."

Brian raised an eyebrow. "And why do you say that?"

"Because I can tell you have issues."

"Oh you can, can you? And what makes you think that?"

An eerie grin emerged on Jake's face. "I may only be eighteen, Doc, but I can read people pretty well. I can tell that you're hiding something behind that doctor mask."

Brian sat up in his chair, angry. Somehow, this kid was getting to him. "We're here to talk about you, Jake. Our sessions have rules. The first being, we only address *your* needs. Never mine. Is that understood?"

"You're hiding something, Doc. Aren't you?"

"That's enough!" Brian took in a deep breath to calm himself. "It's late, anyway. I think it's time you go."

Jake had a satisfied look on his face as he strutted to the door. "Guess I'll be seeing you, shrink."

"Goodnight, Jake."

Jake shut the door behind him.

Brian collapsed against the wall. His heart raced. Sweat poured down his face. He hurried to his desk and frantically searched for a flask.

Jake's words echoed. *You're hiding something, Doc. Aren't you?*

9

Brian stepped out of the elevator and into the florescent-illuminated garage. His vehicle sat alone in the empty lot. The tall white columns produced shadows on his car. A surge of adrenaline pumped through Brian's veins. He glanced around before unlocking his car door.

Why had his session with Jake frightened him? Never had he been so unnerved by a patient before. He saw similar kids at least four to five times a week. Why was this one any different? Something about Jake disturbed him, and he couldn't deduce its origin.

Brian turned the key and the engine bellowed. A figure appeared next to his window. He jumped; his heart fell to his stomach. He looked again. The night security guard, Bernie, stood to his right. Brian let the window down. "Hi, Bernie."

The security guard placed his hand on Brian's door and leaned in. "Hi, Dr. Manifold. You OK?"

"Yeah, I'm good."

Bernie looked around the lot and back to Brian. "You just seem a bit jumpy, and there's been some strange noises here tonight. I just wanted to make sure you were OK."

Brian shrugged. "I'm fine, really."

"You see anybody out of the ordinary?"

A wave of nausea rolled through his stomach. "Um, I had a patient stay a bit later than usual, but he's gone now."

Bernie stepped back and nodded. "OK, then. See you tomorrow, sir."

"Goodnight," Brian said. He pulled out of the parking lot and turned onto to the main road. His body tensed and he sucked in a deep breath. His pulse still pulsated out of control. *Why am I so on edge? Jake is just like all the other kids. Get a grip.*

Brian flipped on his radio and found a classic rock station. He unrolled the window and inhaled the damp night air. It felt great on his face. He started to relax, but then he remembered his destination.

Home.

His stomach hurt again.

ȣȡ

Ray stared at Danielle across the break room. Why couldn't he get up the nerve to ask her out? It was obvious something existed between them. Never had he felt this attracted towards anyone.

He saw Brian cross past the door and Ray's spirits soured. Maybe now wasn't the time. Keeping his best friend in check was a full time job.

"Are you OK?" Danielle asked Ray.

He glanced up into the beautiful eyes. "Um, sure. Why do you ask?"

She slid into the seat across from him. "You just seem sad."

"Maybe I am."

She looked him in the eye, with a genuine expression of concern. "Is it about Dr. Manifold?"

That surprised him. Was he that transparent? Or had she figured that out from their few conversations about him? "Yeah."

"How's he doing?"

"Not so good." He took a sip of his coffee and sighed. "I'm really worried about him. We used to do everything together before the accident."

"Accident?"

"It's a long story." He took a sip of coffee and sighed. "I just wish I could help him."

Danielle reached out and laid her hand softly on his.

A tingling sensation shot up his arm, but he didn't pull away. "Just remember he's your friend, not your patient."

He met her eyes, again surprised by her. "Yeah, I know." So many people assumed Danielle was shallow. "Blonde bimbo" had been a common description. But the more Ray talked to her, the more he realized the staff of this hospital didn't have a clue.

"You have to give him to God," Danielle added.

He glanced down at her hand and allowed his pinky to wrap hers. "That's what I'm trying to do."

"Then you're doing enough."

Ray locked gazes with her, and for the first time in years wanted to kiss someone.

10

Brian walked in the living room just in time to see Lara open the front door and scream. "Oh no! I missed the bus again."

He walked behind her and kissed the top of her head. "Don't worry; I'm actually on time today. I can drop you off."

"Are you sure, Daddy?" Lara grabbed her backpack from her feet, slammed the door closed and followed her father to the driveway.

"Yes, I'm sure. Why wouldn't I be?" He pulled a small fallen branch from his windshield and pushed a remote to unlock the car door.

"No reason." She climbed in the passenger side, tossed her pack in the back seat and turned to face him. "Do you think you can drop me off on Navaho Road?"

"That's a block away from school," he said, confused.

"Yeah, so."

"Yeah, so? Why would you want me to drop you off a block away from school?"

"No reason," she said and glanced out her window.

Brian stared at the back of her head, unsure what to say. Finally, he turned the key in the ignition and backed out of the driveway.

Neither spoke on the short drive.

About a block away from school, Lara pointed to

the curb. "Here's fine."

He maneuvered the car to the curb and frowned. "You and me. We've always been close, right?"

She faced him and smiled. "Yeah. Of course, Daddy. The closest."

"Then what's going on?"

She leaned over and kissed his cheek. "Nothing, I promise. There's nothing to worry about, OK?" She opened the door and snatched her backpack. "See you tonight."

"Bye." Brian watched as his daughter walked in the direction of her school. His mind spun impossible scenarios. No way was he ready for her to be grown up. She was the one thing left in his world worth living for. If she was too mature to have her old man drop her off at school, that wasn't good.

He pulled back onto the road, his jaw tense, another chunk of his heart stripped away.

కింం

"Hi," Danielle said, as she stepped in the elevator next to Ray.

"Hi." He smiled.

The door closed and emotionally charged tension radiated between them.

He looked especially handsome today in a charcoal suit, striped black shirt and silver tie. His hair was purposely messy and he smelled amazing.

"So, I was thinking—"

She pivoted her head slightly toward him. "Yes?"

"I know this is last minute, but tonight I have tickets to the Civic Center to see a show. Interested?"

Fireworks shot off in her chest. She swallowed to

retain some sort of composure. "Yeah. That'd be great." Danielle focused back on the door, trying to steady her breathing. She had a date with the doctor. "So, you're a cultured man?"

"I don't know about that. The tickets were a gift from a colleague."

The door slid open. She stepped out, and then turned back. "See you tonight, then?"

"Or before." He winked and the door closed behind him.

Danielle practically skipped to her car. She had come down to get a snack from the vending machine. What great timing. Was it possible that just happened? Or ordained by her heavenly Father? She smiled, and then sighed. If only she had a girlfriend to tell— someone she could call up and shriek into the phone, "I have a date with Ray Jensen." But she didn't.

She passed the break room, to the parking lot, climbed in her car, blasted the music and screamed. Now she'd never get any work done today. Maybe it was time to take her break.

❧❦

Brian watched Jake for almost an hour. The young man sat on Brian's couch engrossed in the Bible that lay in his lap. After their encounter the night before, Brian assumed Jake would be willing to talk this morning. "Well, Jake, your hour is almost up. With the progress we were making, I had assumed you'd want to talk today. Are you sure you don't want to continue our conversation from last night?"

"Nah." Jake turned the page, and continued to read.

"You do know that this is the time you should talk to me. Not after hours. Next time I will have to report you." Brian stared at Jake, waiting for a reaction.

"I'd think you'd be stoked that we had such a fatty rap." Jake's boots clanked to the floor.

"I'm sorry. Fatty rap?" Brian raised an eyebrow. *That's a new one.*

"You know, blow. Lay it down." Jake smiled. "Or for you old timers—a groovy talk."

"Very funny," Brian said. "Yes, I was glad that you opened up some, but I'd like you to continue moving forward in your therapy."

"You know, for an atheist, I'm surprised you keep a Bible."

Brian shifted in his chair. "Who said I'm an atheist?"

"I can tell." Jake closed the book and tossed it on the coffee table. "Well, it's been stimulating, Doc. I'll be seeing you."

Brian peered over his glasses. "You still have ten minutes."

"My eyes are tired, and I have nothing to say, other than 'I'll see you next week.'"

"You know, Jake, you'll never get better if you aren't willing to talk."

"Yeah, that's probably true." Jake smirked, and then turned for the door, bumping into Lara.

"Sorry," Lara said averting her eyes.

"No worries." Jake grinned. "What's up, kid?"

Lara peered past him to her dad.

"Goodbye, Jake," Brian said, joining her.

Jake backed out slowly, keeping his eye on her as he did.

When the door shut, Brian said, "Hi Sweetie,

how'd you get here?"

"The trolley." She walked to the couch and perched on its arm. "Hey, if I sit here, will you psychoanalyze me?"

"Very funny, but no." Brian sat below her on the couch.

"Why not? I bet I have tons of secrets that could use therapy."

"Because if you needed counseling you would go to someone you don't know." He cradled her chin in his hand. "Not me."

"Why not? I like you. You're the coolest adult I know."

"Because going to therapy with your father isn't healthy and it would be counter-productive."

"Hmm…that's too bad."

"Why's that?"

"'Cause it'd be free." She giggled.

Brian tickled her side.

"OK, truce." She giggled and squirmed away.

"Why are you here, Lara? Shouldn't you be in school?"

She walked to the window and peeked out the blinds. "The beach looks really pretty from here."

"You're avoiding the question." Brian joined her at the window.

"What? Aren't you happy to see your one-and-only daughter?" She posed with one hand on her hip and the other at her face.

"Yes, Lara, I'm always happy to see you. But I have a full schedule today and you have school."

She turned away and sighed dramatically. "Dad, I just came because I felt bad about this morning."

"It's fine. I understand that you're getting older

and it's not cool to hang out with your dad."

"Don't be ridiculous, Dad. I love being with you. It's just…" She half-grinned. "Someday I'll explain. I'm not ready yet. But I love you, Daddy."

"And I love you, too, sweetheart." He kissed the top of her head.

"Since I'm here, can we hang out?" She grabbed his hand and pouted like she did when she was little.

"I wish." He touched her cheek and mimicked her pout. "Unfortunately, like I said, I have a full schedule. Maybe Saturday we could go out to lunch or something. Would you like that?"

She dropped her gaze to the floor with a real pout. "I guess that would be OK."

The phone interrupted them.

"That's probably my next appointment. You'd better get going."

"OK, I'll see you at home." She kissed his cheek and left.

Brian picked up the phone.

"Your next appointment is here, sir," his secretary said.

"Send her in."

A gangly young woman in her mid-thirties entered.

"Ah, Mrs. Myers. Please be seated."

Brian had counseled Annette Myers for almost three years. She suffered from manic depression and bulimia. Her husband had left her years earlier for another woman and she never recovered.

Mrs. Myers settled on the couch, timid and insecure.

Brian sat across from her, poised with the usual pad and pen.

"So, tell me about your week."

She licked her lips and adjusted her glasses. Breathing deeply, a small tear trickled from her eye. "Not so good, I'm afraid."

Brian reached for the tissue box. "Tell me, Mrs. Myers, why wasn't it a good week?"

She sniffled. "I was cleaning out my garage and I found old"—she inhaled—"pictures of us." And then she burst into tears.

The "ritual" began. Mrs. Myers had exhibited the same breakdown every week since the day he started seeing her. She'd cry and he'd console her; she'd vent and he'd give her homework.

Though Brian wanted her to improve, he had to admit, he secretly found comfort in their weekly routine. The hour soon ended, and he showed Mrs. Myers to the door.

"I can't believe it's time to leave so soon." She managed a slight smile.

"Yes, I'm afraid so, but I'll see you next week."

"Thank you, doctor. You're such an angel." She patted his hand.

"Goodbye, Mrs. Myers."

She started to walk out the door, and then turned back. "Dr. Manifold?"

"Yes?"

"I'll be praying for you."

Brian blinked. "Thanks, but I don't really need prayer."

She shook her head. "I may not be a psychologist, doctor, but I can tell when a soul is hurting. Good day." And she was gone.

Brian didn't have time to digest her words.

The phone rang.

"Yes?" he said. "Send her in."

Krissy entered dressed in a short black dress and her usual four-inch heels.

Brian swallowed and met her at the couch.

Obviously, she was used to having men find her attractive.

"Dr. Manifold, I know I am not on your calendar today, but I needed to talk to you."

"Sure, I have a moment. Have a seat." He motioned for her to sit on the couch, but she remained standing.

"I've decided I'm not crazy, and I don't need a shrink anymore."

"I see. And why do you feel that way?"

She moved gracefully towards him, her hips swaying like a metronome. "I like you, Dr. Manifold. And I really don't want anything to stand in our way."

"I told you, I'm married."

"Yes, you did…" she leaned over and brushed her lips over his. She reached for his glasses, but hesitated. "You remind me of someone."

Brian stepped behind his chair. "Look, I like you too, but you have a boyfriend and I have a wife."

She walked around the back of the chair and caressed his arm with her finger. Her touch sent a chill though-out his body. "I don't care." She leaned and kissed him again.

He didn't resist.

"He's out of jail," she whispered.

Brian tried to clear his head. "Who?"

"My ex, Jake. He's out of jail."

Brian's heart picked up speed. He took a step back. "Jake?"

"Yeah. He was sent away for murdering some

girl."

Brian felt weak. *Jake? My Jake?* "You need to go."

Krissy pouted. "Ah, come on, doc. Don't let Jake bother you. He's harmless."

"He killed a woman. And he's a—" Patient confidentiality stopped him from finishing his statement.

Krissy swiped at the air. "He didn't mean to do it. It just happened. Besides, he's a child. I want a man." She moved toward him again.

Brian recoiled. "Look, really. You've got to go," he said firmly. "I really need you to."

She stared at him, obviously weighing her chances. Finally, she shrugged her shoulders and sauntered toward the door with a confused expression painting her pretty face. "Goodbye, Dr. Manifold. Come see me if you change your mind. You know where I live."

The office fell silent, but his head was screaming. Brian walked to his drawer and poured himself a drink. *What have I done?*

⇛⇚

With the exception of his encounter with Danielle in the elevator, Ray dreaded this morning. He had to talk to Brian, and it wouldn't be pleasant. He entered Brian's office, unsure if he was ready for this encounter. How he wished God could get through to his friend, so life could continue the way it used to be. "Good, I'm glad to see you're still here."

Brian rolled his eyes, and then stared back at his notes.

"And as usual, you're not as glad to see me." Ray

walked to the couch. "Please join me. We need to talk."

"And you wonder why I'm never happy to see you." Brian busied himself with tidying his desk. "What's up, Ray? I need to get going."

"I came to see how you're doing."

"I'm fine," he said.

"Are you sure?"

Brian let out an exasperated sigh.

"The custodians mentioned someone yelling in your office the other night, and I thought I'd check to make sure you're OK."

"I'm fine. Jake has some anger issues that we're trying to work through, but I really don't think he'd hurt me."

"Jake?"

Brian realized he had given up the patient's identity. "Sorry, I shouldn't have revealed his name."

"You know I have access to all your patients' files, anyway." Ray stepped in front of the desk with crossed arms. "How did Jake get in the hospital after hours?"

"I don't know. I guess I should have asked, but he hasn't opened up, yet, and seemed desperate to talk to someone." Brian shifted in his chair. "I guess my main focus was on that."

Ray rubbed his chin, trying to think that through. "But why after hours?"

Brian shrugged. "I don't know."

Ray nodded. "Well, you should be getting home. We'll talk about this more later."

Brian rolled his eyes again. "I can't wait."

"Goodnight, Brian."

❧

Ray sat at his desk, writing his report. Dr. Jai was breathing down his neck for some explanation into Brian's bizarre conduct. Ray didn't have enough details yet, but he was beginning to fear the worst.

When he turned in this report, Brian would never forgive him. The hope of a renewed friendship between them would cease to exist. Why did things have to be this way? In college, they were the best of friends—ready to change the world. Of course, back then their only real problem was which girl to ask out to their next fraternity event.

Nothing good would happen now. Ray sighed. All of Brian's patients' files sat in front of him. He hoped they would give him some insight into his friend's odd behavior. Ray touched the corner of the first file. His stomach flipped. He was afraid of what he might uncover. It was out of true friendship that he'd volunteered to take Brian's case. If there was something unpleasant to discover, he wanted to be the first to know. Ray grabbed a pen from inside his jacket and wrote "Jake" on the top of a yellow steno pad on his desk. He would start there.

The cell phone in his jacked buzzed. He snapped it open.

"Hi," Danielle said.

Oh no. "Danielle, hi."

"I was just checking. We're still on tonight, right?"

He glanced at his watch. "I really wanted to take you out, but something came up here. I hope you won't kill me, but can I ask for a rain check?"

It took a moment for her to answer, and Ray dreaded that she might be angry.

"Um, sure. No problem. I'll just see you Monday, then?"

"Sounds good. I really am sorry. Thanks for understanding."

"Yeah. Goodnight."

"Goodnight." He snapped his phone closed, and walked to a counter on the side of the room. He hoped she wasn't too mad. He really liked her. This wasn't about him taking her out, though he had to admit, it did frighten him.

No, this was about the task at hand—Brian's future. That frightened him even more. He flipped the switch on the coffee pot and it hissed. It would be a late night—he'd need his caffeine.

⁊∘⊰

Danielle sat on the bed, surrounded by outfits, cradling the phone. She couldn't move. Her heart hurt too much. All day she'd glammed up for this night, including several hours to get her hair and nails done. She bought a gorgeous black dress and killer matching pumps. She glanced to her left at her reflection in the mirror. Never had she looked this beautiful, and it was for naught. She might as well go into work and make up the hours she took off.

She unzipped her dress and let it fall around her ankles. *Why Lord? Why must I always be in love with the guys who are emotionally unavailable?* She didn't doubt that he was busy. He'd made it clear that Dr. Manifold was a huge priority. But that didn't change the fact that he had stood her up.

She pulled on a pair of scrubs and grabbed a chocolate bar from the fridge. Tonight, she'd need chocolate. It was the only thing that could sooth her broken heart.

11

Ray stared at the cantaloupes, unsure what a ripe one looked like. His mother kept harassing him about eating more fruit. Did he even like melon? It sounded good. He reached for the tan ball.

"Dr. Jensen?"

Ray spun around, and his heart leapt. "Danielle." She looked different. No makeup, her hair pulled back by a hair clip, and she wore gray sweats. *Still beautiful.* "So, what are you doing here?" OK, that was a stupid question. "Besides shopping?"

"Getting dinner, actually. I tend to eat for one, so if I shop a week at a time..."

"It all goes bad," he finished.

She nodded, and laughed. "Exactly."

He looked into his empty cart filled with two frozen dinners and a pair of apples. "Well, I'm attempting to do the same thing, but as you can see, I'm clueless."

She nodded with an amused expression.

"I guess I still owe you dinner," he said.

A slow smile crossed her lips. "Yes, I believe you do."

"I'm not much of a cook, but—"

"So, why don't you come over to my place? I'm making orange chicken and wild rice."

He lifted the frozen Salisbury steak from his cart. "I don't know. It's kind of hard to beat this."

She laughed. "I insist. I just need to grab a few more things, and we can go."

❧❧

Danielle placed orange slices on the plates, took a deep breath, and walked them into the living room.

Ray sat behind a TV tray reading a newspaper.

She couldn't believe that he was here, in her house, reading her paper, and about to eat her food. This seemed surreal. Only last night she wasted precious tears on a confirmed failure of this dream, but now here he sat. For a second, she almost imagined what it would be like to be a married woman making her man dinner.

He folded the paper down and smiled. "Mmm, smells wonderful."

She handed him a fork and napkin, and then joined him on the couch. "Sorry, I don't have a dining set. I tend to eat while watching television."

"So you really are a nerd."

She frowned. No one had called her that since high school.

He laughed. "I meant that in the most endearing way. I do the same thing."

Not meeting his gaze, she grinned and reached for the remote. "Then you won't mind if I put it on now?" She wasn't really in the mood to watch it; she just needed something to calm the tension in the room. Electricity or discomfort, she hadn't decided. She really liked him, but wasn't sure how much of that was returned.

"Sounds good." He picked up his fork and brought some rice to his mouth. "Mmm, much better than a frozen dinner."

"Thanks."

While they ate, their conversation lingered on the show in front of them. A whale had found himself stuck in the San Diego bay. Researchers debated over whether they should help him back to the open waters, or just let him be.

"Seriously, if he wants to stay in the bay, why don't they let him?" Danielle said.

"He could get hurt," Ray replied.

"Well, sometimes nature has to be nature, you know?"

He smiled at her, studying her.

It sent a shock wave to her heart.

When they'd finished their food, she stood to clear the plates. At the same time, he stood. Their faces were less than an inch apart. Her heart pounded. She swallowed, wanting so much for him to touch his lips to hers.

Instead, he dropped his gaze to his pocket, and lifted out a vibrating cell phone. "Excuse me."

"Of course." She nodded and reached for the plates. Not that she really felt it was "OK." She wanted that kiss. Couldn't he have ignored the call, even for a second? Then she scolded herself for being so selfish. He was a psychologist. Always on call, as were most of the people at work. She knew when the phone rang, they took the call. If she wanted to date a doctor, she'd have to get used to that.

Date a doctor. She set the dishes in the sink and sighed.

"I'm afraid I have to go," he said from the kitchen doorway.

"I understand." She forced a smile, and reached

for a packaged fruit pie. "Here, dessert. You like cherry?"

"Love cherry." He laughed and took it. "Thank you for dinner. It was wonderful."

"You're welcome."

With a tight grin, he nodded, and then left.

What am I doing? She ripped open a chocolate pudding pie and leaned her hip against the counter. Maybe putting her heart out there wasn't the best idea. Too often, she'd been hurt. But she really liked him. *Lord, if this is dumb, tell me.*

෧ఞ

Ray hurried to his car. The call hadn't been that important. His mom wanted him to call his Aunt Willie and wish her a happy birthday. So, why did he run? There he sat in the home of a beautiful woman; someone he clearly had feelings for, and he'd bolted. *I really am a dweeb.*

He stared up at her apartment and sighed. A part of him said to go back up there and be a man. Ask the girl out on a real date. The other part, the part that was winning, kept him glued to his leather interior.

He was thirty-seven years old and not getting any younger. Though he never hurt for the watchful eyes of women, he hardly cared much. He was married to his job. But Danielle did something to him. It unnerved him. He went the long way to his office every day, just to see her apple-red lips smile at him. How lame was that?

No one would guess the truth. He was scared to death of women, always had been. Sure, he carried himself like a man with confidence, but inside he was a gooey marshmallow.

Maybe that was why he'd been a mama's boy for so long. Mom was easy. He knew how to talk to her. But in the last few years, he'd pulled away from her, and now realized he hated being alone.

For a while, Brian's issues filled his time and concentration. And even now, he often used that as an excuse.

But he couldn't deny it any longer. He desired to be more than just a friend to Danielle.

He squeezed his eyes shut and pushed all the air from his lungs. *Just go back up there.* Butterflies danced in his stomach. He grabbed the handle on his car door, just as his cell phone rang.

He glanced at the display. Saved by the bell. This wasn't a call he could ignore.

12

Brian pulled into the circular driveway and stared up at the two-story white stucco house that cost him a half-million dollars. A home any family would love to own. Big bay windows, a three-car garage, four bedrooms, a loft. Yes, it was the perfect house. And yet, to Brian, its walls imprisoned him.

He pulled a flask from inside his suit pocket and slowly unscrewed the cap. A chuckle welled inside him and he laughed aloud. His voice echoed loudly in the silent car, but he couldn't seem to control it. Nothing was funny. Was he losing his mind?

His laughter turned to anger. He stared at the house with disdain. Only a small porch light lit the house. Its walls mocked him.

"I hate you! I haaaate you!" he yelled to the dismal dwelling. He took a swig from the container and let the liquid sit in his mouth until he almost gagged. Squinting, he forced it down his throat. His eyes watered.

Someone tapped on his window.

Brian's heart leapt.

"Dad, open the door!" Lara yelled from outside his window.

Brian stuffed the flask under his seat and unlocked the door.

"Hi, honey," he slurred, stepping out of his car. His legs wobbled and he fell against her.

"Dad, you're drunk! You could have killed someone."

"Shh! You're going to wake the neighbors. Just help me inside."

Lara wrapped his arm around her neck and kicked the car door closed with her foot. Unable to support his weight, they both fell into the bushes lining the walkway.

"Are you OK?" she asked.

"Fine. You?" He pushed himself back up.

Lara moved in position to help him again. "Dad, why are you doing this to yourself?"

"You're young. You'll understand when you're older."

Lara pushed open the front door.

Brian staggered through and patted the wall for the light switch.

"Here." Lara flipped the hall light on and helped Brian sit on the bottom stair. "Dad, this isn't helping you. You need to talk to Mom."

"Stop it!" He looked her in the eye. "Stop badgering me about talking to your mother. She brought this on herself. If she would just get over it and move on—"

"Are you over everything?" Lara cocked her head to the side. "Because if you are, you sure don't act like it."

"I'm fine. I'm going on with life. That's what she should do, too."

Lara shook her head and sat next to her father. "This isn't going on with life. This is walking towards an early death. I think you need help."

"Enough! You're my daughter. You don't have a right to talk to me like this. Do you hear me?" Brian held onto the railing and tried to stand. "Now, go to bed. You have school in the morning."

"Tomorrow is Saturday."

Brian folded back to the stairs, his head pressed into the white metal handrail. He relaxed and let his body slide down the steps. His head hit the last rung.

"Dad, are you OK?"

He didn't answer.

"Daddy?"

Still didn't answer.

"I'll get Mom." Lara headed for the master bedroom.

"No!" he snapped. Brian opened his eyes and sighed. "Look, I'm fine. I just hate the weekend."

Lara stopped and faced him. "How can you hate the weekend? Everybody loves time off."

Brian pushed himself away from the railing and placed his head between his knees. "Not me."

"Are you sure you're OK?"

"Didn't I tell you to go to your room?"

"Yeah."

Brian looked unsteadily at her. "Then I suggest you go."

"But— "

"Go."

"Yes, Daddy." She kissed the top of his head and trudged up the stairs behind him.

Brian lay sprawled out over five steps. It wasn't comfortable, so he allowed himself to slide to the cream colored tile below. When his head hit the floor, he winced in pain. He didn't care. Tomorrow was Saturday. That meant a whole two days with his catatonic wife.

Ray watched from down the street. Brian was a mess. He could barely walk straight. *Hopefully, Rhonda won't ever be awake to see him like this.* His heart ached for his friend. Should he stay longer?

He glanced at the cherry pie on the seat next to him, and smiled. Danielle was something else. He hated that he had to leave her. Maybe he'd imagined it, but they'd almost kissed. Going back up there would have been good, but he'd received the call, and a promise was a promise. Watching over Brian had become a fulltime job. Until things were better, he had no choice.

The cell rang in his pocket. He snapped it open. "Dr. Jensen."

"You can go now. Thank you."

"Anytime." He snapped the phone closed. His job here was done.

"You're not going to make it." The sinister voice slinked through the darkness. A soft, smoke-like cloud hovered in the streets and a small shaft of light filtered from a distant lamppost.

Brian rubbed his head. *Where am I? More important, how did I get here?*

He glanced down at his clothes. He still wore the blue suit he'd worn all day, and a raincoat he didn't recognize. He strained to see. *I must be in an alley somewhere downtown.* Barefoot and cold, he moved toward the light.

"You're not going to make it."

The chilling declaration iced Brian's blood. His heart pounded. The air lay like bricks in his lungs. "Who said that?"

Silence.

"Who's there?"

Brian leaned against a damp cement wall. Sweat dripped from his hair and stung his eyes.

"You're not going to make it."

"Stop saying that!"

"You're not...going...to make it."

Brian shrieked. He stumbled into a run, heading for the light. He tripped over his trench coat and landed face down on the pavement. His forehead burned. Warm liquid seeped down his face and into his mouth. Brian touched his cheek. *Blood.*

"You're not going to make it, Brian!" It knew *his* name.

Brian pushed himself up, but fell again. His legs would not support him. He put his hands in front of his body and pulled himself—his legs dragging behind—down the street. He peeked over his shoulder, but only night followed.

When he turned back toward the light, he stopped.

Someone or something blocked his way.

Brian squinted. It appeared to be an enormous creature with a body like an ogre and a face that resembled a dragon. Its long, spiny claws clicked on the ground with each step. The vile beast breathed amber smoke from its nostrils and russet ooze dripped from its crimson eyes.

Brian lay crying like a small child. He covered his head with his arms, unable to face the awful creature. "What do you want from me?"

"I *have* it," hissed the beast.

"What? What do you have?"

"Your soul, Brian. Give up. You're not going to make it." Again, those haunting words.

Silence.

Brian peered through the cracks between his fingers. The beast was gone. Brian tried to stand. His legs wobbled like rubber. He squeezed his eyes closed to try to clear his mind. When he opened his eyes, he heard breathing in the darkness.

I'm in bed? It was only a dream. A nightmare. But he didn't feel any better. Instead, he felt that familiar pain in the pit of his stomach. How could he get rid of the anguish that resided in his heart? He didn't know how much longer he could continue living in this way.

Afraid to return to the nightmare, Brian stared at the ceiling until the sun streamed through the blinds.

❧❦

"Lara!" Brian yelled at the top of the stairs. "Are you awake?"

Brian could hear scurrying around on the other side of the door. The knob turned and Lara peeked out. "Dad?" she asked, half-awake.

"Hi, honey. Want to go get some pancakes?"

Lara groaned. She glanced over her shoulder at the clock on the wall, and then back to her dad. "It's six in the morning."

"I know," Brian smiled. "And I want pancakes."

Lara rolled her eyes.

"Come on. It's Saturday. We could get a bite to eat, and then I'll drop you off anywhere you want to go. Think about it. You won't have to ride the trolley to go see your friends."

Lara seemed to consider that before answering. "Fine, but give me a minute." She shut the door.

Brian grinned. If there was one thing left to smile about, it was that young lady. After his nightmare last night, he figured it was time to put his energy somewhere that made sense. And she made sense.

Brian sat on the bottom stair and ran his hands through his hair. He started to close his eyes, when he heard her bound down the stairs behind him.

She wore a pale yellow dress, and a daisy in her hair.

"That's pretty. Where'd you get it?"

"You bought it, don't you remember?"

Brian shrugged. "Nope. Ready?"

"Yeah." She nodded. "Did you say goodbye to Mom?"

Brian's smile faded. "Yes, not that it did any good. Come on, let's go."

❧❦

Brian sat across from Lara at *Trucker's Diner*. She nibbled on pancakes, while he packed them in. He stopped mid-bite. "What?" he asked through his stuffed mouth.

"You've been acting weird since we got here." She glanced around.

"Don't be silly." He grabbed his milk and swallowed.

"Stop smiling. It's unnerving."

He set down his fork and dabbed his mouth with a napkin. "I'm happy to be with you. What's wrong with that?"

"For weeks you've been a mess, and now, you

won't stop baring your teeth for everyone to see." She grimaced at a woman dressed in a Hawaiian dress who was sitting at the bar. "People are staring."

"So, let them look," Brian said, taking another forkful of maple-covered dough into his mouth. "I'm having a good time with my daughter. So what?"

"But dad, you're acting like a nut. Who holds a smile that long? You look like a creepy Cheshire cat."

"Don't be ridiculous." Brian waved his hand, and then pointed to her untouched plate of food. "Aren't you going to eat?"

She shook her head. "Nah. I'm not hungry."

Brian licked the last morsel from his dish and grabbed her plate. "Then I guess you won't mind if I eat yours?"

Lara buried her head in her hands. "You can be so embarrassing."

"So, how's school?" he asked between bites.

"Great."

"I haven't heard anything from the school, so I just wondered, that's all."

"I'm fine." Lara stared down at her hands, her sullen expression revealing anything but "fine."

"Do you want to talk about it?"

"No, I just want to get out of here."

He finished his coffee and grabbed the check from the corner of the table. "Are you ready?"

"Yes, please."

He tossed a few bills under his plate. "Then let's get out of here."

"Finally," she said.

He hugged her as they went to the exit, all eyes on them.

13

Danielle spent the entire weekend hoping Ray would call. So stupid. This wasn't high school, and she wasn't a pubescent teenager waiting for a boy to dial her digits.

Monday morning she went to work early and ducked in the staff restroom. Today, Ray couldn't avoid her. Maybe, just maybe, he'd actually ask her out. She touched a smear of gloss at the corner of her lip and sighed. *A girl can hope.*

"Morning," Sheila said behind her in the mirror.

Danielle smiled. "Hi." The entire time Danielle had worked here, this had to be the first time Dr. Manifold's secretary had actually talked to her. "You're here early, too?"

"I have a few things to do before Dr. Dread arrives." She stepped to the sink and washed her hands.

"Dr. Dread?"

The woman pinched her lips together, obviously having shared more than she meant to. "Sorry, things have been a bit tense, lately. I forgot you and Brian are, um, friends." She cleared her throat.

Danielle held up her hand. "We're not friends."

Sheila raised an eyebrow.

Great. Even his secretary thought the horrid rumor was true. "I barely know the man. Whatever you've heard is incorrect. I promise."

She snatched a paper towel from the silver holder on the wall. "Be glad. It can't be easy to be his friend. I feel bad for Dr. Jensen."

Danielle's heart fluttered at Ray's name. "Why do you say that? Because Dr. Manifold has been drunk a few times on the job?"

"Ha!" Sheila huffed. "If only it was that simple. That is only the icing, my dear. Being that man's friend must be exhausting. I can't even imagine."

Now Danielle was curious. She'd noticed some odd behavior from Brian, but this sounded worse. "Why? What else has he done?"

The door opened.

"I've got to get back." Sheila turned away quickly, tossed her trash in the can, and exited.

How was Brian's behavior affecting Ray, beyond what she already knew? Curiosity would eat away at her until she had an answer. Sheila wasn't the kind of woman to openly approach Danielle again. And they didn't exactly run in the same circles.

She walked to the bathroom door, hoping maybe her boss or someone else knew something. But how would she find out, without gossiping? She tossed the trash and made her way back to her desk.

"Good morning," Ray said.

Danielle blinked and composed a smile. "Oh, hello, doctor."

"I'm sorry about leaving so soon the other night," he whispered.

She shrugged. "I'm sure it comes with the job."

"Yes." He scratched at a pen mark on the counter, not looking her in the eye. "Maybe we can try again sometime."

"I'd like that."

"How about—"

The elevator door opened and Dr. Manifold exited. Ray frowned. "If you'll excuse me."

"Sure," she said, disappointed.

Ray walked across the lobby and said something to his friend. Whatever it was, Brian didn't seem happy and stormed away. Hot on his heels, Ray followed. They disappeared down the hall, out of sight.

"I'm glad you're here early. Can you file these?" Merle asked, stacking a pile of folders on the counter.

Danielle exhaled slowly. Time to put her heart and curiosity away and get to work.

∂∞§

After finally getting rid of Ray, Brian decided he needed a drink. He served himself a cup of half coffee, half bourbon, downed it, and then poured another. By the fourth cup, he'd dismissed the coffee.

Sheila poked her head in the door.

"Ah, Sheila," Brian slurred. "What can I do for you?"

She eyed him suspiciously. "Do you want to go over your calendar for the week?"

Brian smiled lazily and waved her over to the couch as he meandered to his chair. Crossing his legs, he beckoned her. "Go ahead."

With a furrowed brow, she sat and opened the calendar. She started to address the schedule, but stopped and peered back at him. "Aren't you going to get your calendar?"

Brian glanced back at his desk and chuckled. "Yeah, I guess that would make sense, wouldn't it?" He finished off his drink and grabbed his planner.

"OK, I guess I'm ready now."

"Are you sure? Because I can always come back later."

Brian shook his head and ignored her sarcasm. "No, you go right ahead."

Sheila sighed and turned to her calendar. "Tuesday you have 9:00 AM with Tony Ashcroft; 10:30 with Myra Briggs; 3:00 PM with... "

Brian closed his eyes, and plastered a goofy grin on his face.

She sighed dramatically. "Dr. Manifold, are you even listening to me?"

He knew she was irritated, but he didn't care.

The leather on the sofa exhaled as she shifted her weight.

He peeked out through his eyelashes and giggled.

"Unbelievable!" She got up and stormed out of his office.

Brian opened his eyes and started to laugh uncontrollably. The hilarity took over his body, causing tears to spill down his face. Sheila could probably hear him at her desk, and for that reason alone, he knew he should stop. But the more he tried to get control, the harder he laughed.

❧

It was barely eight o'clock in the morning, and Ray sat in a room filled with employees from all different status levels. The custodian shared a couch with the head of administration. Everybody had a complaint. Some were worried, others angry. The subject of their concern? Dr. Brian Manifold.

"I've had it!" Sheila snapped. "It's not right! He

shouldn't be allowed to go on working as a licensed psychologist. If you don't do something soon, I'll quit. I won't have a drunk doctor's behavior on my conscience."

Ray nodded. What more could he do? He loved Brian, but they were right. Something had to be done. "I understand your concerns. Trust me, I'm looking into it. I suggest you jot down some of your experiences with Dr. Manifold and I'll put them in my report." Ray paced toward the door. "Now, if you'll all excuse me, I have a meeting with Dr. Jai in a few minutes to discuss this."

The group stood in unison and muttered their way out the door and down the hall.

Ray sighed.

The bonfire had just inflamed into an inferno.

❧

Brian stood in line at the hospital cafeteria, uneasy.

The staff he'd encountered greeted him with plastic smiles and hurried hellos. *Has everyone gone mad?*

"Tuna on rye," he said to the woman behind the counter.

Danielle grabbed a tray behind him. Happy to see a friend, Brian turned to her and smiled. "Danielle, how have you been?"

She looked up, startled. "Oh, Dr. Manifold. I didn't see you there."

"Brian," he said correcting her.

"Right." She grabbed a salad from the case. "Oh, um...I've been fine. How are *you*?"

Brian peered around the room at the spectators.

"I've been better." He leaned closer to her and lowered his voice. "Is it just me, or is everyone acting weird?"

She laughed nervously and followed his gaze. "Um…if you'll excuse me. I need to…I forgot to…I've got to go." She returned the salad to the case and retreated.

Baffled, Brian watched her white heels click hastily down the hallway. "Has everyone gone nuts?"

"That's all in how you look at it," Ray said from behind. He turned to the lady behind the counter. "Turkey sandwich on whole wheat, hold the mayo." Then to Brian, he added, "Mom is making me watch my cholesterol. I guess my last check up scared her."

Brian handed the cashier a five. "Don't you think you're a little old to care what Mommy thinks?"

The woman reached out to hand him a quarter.

"Keep it." Brian made a beeline to a booth by the window away from the majority of onlookers.

A moment later, Ray joined him.

"You can't resist, can you?" Brian asked.

"Resist what?" Ray set his tray down.

"Torturing me."

Ray grinned. "Look, I won't bother you long. I just have to ask you something."

Brian rolled his eyes. "What?"

"Have you been drinking on the job?"

Heat flooded Brian's face. He slammed his hand on the table, and a saltshaker toppled over. "I'm on my lunch break, Ray. Give it a rest, OK?"

Ray sighed. "Fine. But do you see all these people staring at you?"

Brian quickly glanced over his shoulder, and then back at Ray. "Yeah, what's their deal, anyway?"

"They've all registered complaints against you."

Heat rose up Brian's spine, and his heart accelerated. "Complaints about me? Why?"

"They claim you drink on the job, yell at clients, miss and cancel appointments, are constantly late, snap at your fellow workers for no reason, talk to…"

"Enough!" Brian yelled, bounding out of his seat. He grabbed his tray and tossed his untouched sandwich in the trash. "Thanks for a stimulating lunch break, Ray." Then he turned to the open room and fanned out his arms. "Sign them all up, Doc. Your staff is obviously in need of some serious therapy."

❧

Brian plodded off down the hall.

Ray had pushed Brian in hopes that it would help, not hurt. He needed Brian to see the reality of his actions. But he now realized that Brian existed in a world of denial.

The people in the room stared at Ray, all with the same "I told you so" expressions exhibited across their faces. He nodded, head bowed. He didn't really feel like eating, either. He would turn in his report, and Brian would be fired. If only Ray could help him. But it was too late now.

"Are you OK?"

He looked up into the most gorgeous and welcoming eyes. "Danielle."

"May I?" She pointed to the seat across from him.

"Of course."

She slid in and reached out to touch his hand. A shot of electricity went up his arm. He worked to block it out. Now was not the time. He slowly withdrew his hand and glanced around the room.

She looked, too, obviously realizing how inappropriate that would appear in here. "I saw what happened, and I'm sorry."

"He's my friend."

"I know." She sighed. "How can I help you?"

Defeat hung heavy on his shoulders. He allowed his gaze to meet hers. The concern there was genuine. "Thank you."

"For what?"

"For being a friend to me."

Her gaze dropped to the table.

"Did I say something wrong?"

She shook her head. "No, I'd just like to be more than a friend to you."

He swallowed, not sure what to say. Of course, he wanted that too, but now?

She raised her head slowly.

A force he hadn't felt in years drew him to her. Chemistry held them like a blanket. He licked his lips, unable to pull his stare from hers. This was stupid. Really dumb. The cafeteria was filled with gossipers. He inched closer. The smell of vanilla filtered to his nose.

"Excuse me, sir," his secretary, Elena said.

He jumped back and cleared his throat. "Yes, Elena?"

She glanced from him to Danielle, and then back to him. "I'm sorry to disturb you on your break, but you have that important call you asked for."

He understood. It was *she*.

∽∾

The minute Ray was out of sight, Danielle buried

her head in her arms. *Oh my goodness*. If she could scream this second, she would. It was as if some invisible force kept pulling them apart. *Lord, is this You? Because if it is, then I need You to take this ache in my heart away. I like him too much.*

But part of her knew this wasn't the ideal time for Ray to be starting a relationship. Maybe God was protecting them. A relationship started under these circumstances would end badly. Right now what Ray needed was a friend, someone to help him walk through everything with Brian.

She frowned. This had been her chance to get Ray to open up about Brian's behavior, and instead she was baring her soul.

"You eating?"

Danielle sat up and sighed. "Yeah, Merle, I suppose I should grab something."

"You look tired. Maybe you should clock out early tonight."

Maybe she should. "I'll think about it."

"Good." Merle slid across from her and opened a bagged lunch. "I don't trust the food here. You want some of my homemade chicken bake?"

Danielle stared at the red plastic dish and smiled. Anything to get her mind off where it had been. "Sure. I'd love some."

❧❦

Brian had gone to three bars before heading home. At least in the company of the inebriated, he was free from death stares.

Driving home now, he mulled over his day, and honestly couldn't come up with a sound reason why the staff had turned on him. Especially Danielle. They had flirted on several occasions, and she'd always been nice to him.

Work was Brian's safe place, the one place where he felt normal. Now it was turning into another prison.

He pulled into his driveway and stumbled out of the car. From the corner of his eye, he caught something glimmer. He squinted in the dark, barely making out the silhouette of a car at the end of the cul-de-sac. His house was the last house, and usually didn't have any traffic. Maybe it was nothing. He shrugged and swaggered up the steps.

Brian's hand shook. He worked to get the key in the door. The car down the street turned on its lights and Brian stopped. He shaded his eyes, but the car didn't move. Brian staggered backwards to the lawn. His foot hit a sprinkler head and he fell to the ground. When he stood up, the car was gone.

I must be seeing things. He moved back to the door. He fumbled with his keys, and managed to unlock the door and step inside. The house sat serenely still. He closed the door and crossed to his bedroom, slipped off his shoes and fell into bed. He pulled the covers to his chin and edged his eyes closed. The room spun like the teacups ride at a carnival. Breathing deep, he labored to relax.

His stomach turned over. Brian lunged out of bed and made a dash for the toilet, just in time to be rid of the drink in his system. He lay back at the edge of the porcelain throne and tried to recall happier times.

His mind drifted to when he met Rhonda. It was the first day of the spring semester and she was working part-time at the campus coffee shop at San Diego Christian College.

Her dark, shiny hair fell to her waist and her emerald-green eyes seemed to look right into a person's soul. Every Wednesday night for three months, he sat at her table and ordered a black coffee and a glazed donut. He thought she was pretty, but never gave her a second thought.

Mainly because Brian thought he loved a blonde who sang in the chorale. Funny, he couldn't even remember the blonde's name now.

Rhonda made the first move. While pouring his coffee, she invited him to a poetry reading on campus.

Brian needed the credit for a humanities project and agreed to go.

Rhonda was scheduled to read that night. By the last line of her sonnet, he'd forgotten the blonde.

They'd dated only two months when he'd asked her to marry him. A year before he entered grad school, they got married.

She had worked hard to support him during those times, and he promised her that when he was a doctor, she could go back to school and stay home with their kids. That was the plan. And then...

Brian spit in the toilet. He didn't know what hurt worse, his stomach or his heart. He grabbed a wad of tissue and wiped at his face. "If onlys" raced through his mind. He used the edge of the tub to push up, and then walked back to his bed.

Leaning against the headboard, he stared at Rhonda sleeping. His beautiful wife appeared so lost. He hated "if onlys." They never accomplished anything. They always came too late.

Rhonda's rhythmic breathing stopped. She got out of bed, walked to the bathroom and flipped on the light switch.

Am I dreaming? Brian sat gaping at the silhouette in the doorway.

She closed the door.

Why am I so surprised? Rhonda must go to the bathroom from time to time. Right? She must eat, too. Why hadn't he seen it before? Brian sat up and turned on the lamp by the bed. He noticed a small Bible and a highlighter sitting on her side. That wasn't there before, was it?

Maybe Rhonda was doing better. Maybe the lurid dream was finally over. He couldn't wait for her to come back to bed. He would finally get to talk to her.

He stared at the door. Only the ticking of the living room clock punctuated the night. *What's taking her so long?* The glow from under the door was the only indication that she was even there.

He waited.

Nothing.

He walked to the door and knocked. "Honey, are you all right?"

No response.

"Rhonda?"

Brian opened the door and gasped. Rhonda lay in the bathtub covered in blood. He rushed to the side of the tub and grabbed her.

"Rhonda!"

"It's too late, Brian," she said in a barely audible voice.

"No, it can't be. This is my fault. If only… "

Rhonda rubbed his hand with hers. "Call the hospital."

Brian nodded. He walked to the phone by their bed, but he couldn't see the buttons through his tears. He wiped at his face with his sleeve and punched 911.

Shaking, he fell to the floor.

"This is the 911 Operator. What is your emergency?"

Brian croaked. "I've killed her."

14

Danielle shot up in bed, gasping. It took her a moment to clearly determine where she was. The nightmare she'd just walked through made her heart race. She imagined an enormous beast chasing someone. She couldn't make out the face, but it felt so real.

She sank down slowly, and took a gulp of air to calm her nerves. Her heart slowly settled, but her spirit did not. For some reason, she felt like praying. Not for anything in particular, her soul just needed it. A heavy burden lingered in the room, causing her unrest. *Dear Lord, I don't know what troubles me. Maybe it was that dream, or maybe it is something more. I pray, in your name, for peace for whoever that was. For whatever troubles me now.* She closed her eyes and continued to pray. Eventually, she fell back to sleep.

❧❦

The early morning sunlight glistened between the cracks in the blinds and into Brian's eyes. For some reason he lay sprawled out on the bedroom floor. He squinted at the bathroom door and his heart fell into his stomach. Brian jumped up, snatched open the door, and peered across the small room. The tub lay empty.

What? Brian turned around.

Rhonda slept peacefully on the bed.

"Rhonda?"

She didn't answer.

"Rhonda, are you awake?"

Still silence.

Confused by the obscure dream, he undressed for the shower.

"Brian?"

His stomach leapt. He turned around slowly.

Rhonda sat up.

"Rhonda? You're awake?"

"Brian, we need to talk."

Brian rushed to her side and took her in his arms. "I'm so sorry, Rhonda. So very sorry."

"I know."

Brian pulled back. "Where have you been?"

Rhonda's eyebrows furrowed. "What do you mean?"

Brian shook his head. "I mean, while you lay there sleeping, what do you think about?"

Her face remained blank.

"Well, we can talk about it later. I need to get to work. I'm glad you're awake. We'll talk tonight, OK?"

Rhonda nodded.

He kissed her cheek, grabbed a beige towel from the hall pantry, and walked in the bathroom. He closed the door and smiled at his reflection. His dark eyes appeared haggard. *Well, of course they do, I've been living a nightmare—both awake and asleep.*

Brian reached behind the glass door and turned the knob. He stepped in the shower and let the warm water spill over his face. He couldn't help but beam. Things were getting better. He just knew it.

She's awake.

෩෨

Brian couldn't believe he willingly stepped into an elevator and pushed the button to the seventh floor of St. Ruth's hospital. He avoided the administrative floor like one avoided shots. Even more surprising was his reason for going. With the recent change in Rhonda, Brian needed someone to confide in and Ray was the only one who really knew his wife.

Brian peeked his head in Ray's office and rapped on the door jamb.

Ray looked up from his laptop. "Brian," he said. "What a surprise!"

"Are you busy?"

"No more than usual. Come on in." Ray motioned to the chairs in the center of the office. "Have a seat."

Brian moved to the end of Ray's desk and sat in one of the brown overstuffed chairs. "I have good news."

"Really? What's that?"

"Rhonda and I spoke this morning."

"That's wonderful. I know there's been a lot of tension since the accident." Ray smiled and joined Brian in the facing chair. "What did you talk about?"

"Nothing, really. It's just so good to hear her voice again."

"I guess its progress that you talked to her," Ray said.

"I think its progress that she talked at all. I was beginning to think I'd have to call the mental hospital to pick her up."

Ray cocked his head to the side and stared at Brian.

"What?" Brian asked annoyed.

"Rhonda said the same about you."

Brian's eyes went wide. "When?"

"She's been saying it for months."

"What?" Brian jumped to his feet. "You've been talking to her?"

Ray looked confused. "Of course."

Brian's cheeks burned red. "You mean it's all been an act?"

"Calm down, Brian."

Brian paced like a trapped lion. "How could she do that to me? Here I'm about to lose my mind and she was talking to my best friend the whole time." Brian stared at Ray, anger eating his soul. "No! My back-stabbing boss!" Then before he could stop his lips from moving, he asked, "Are you two having an affair?"

Ray's face turned red. "What?" he snapped. "Don't be ridiculous!"

"Am I?"

Ray shook his head. "If you knew your wife, then you'd know better than to ask me that. Go home, Brian. Take some time off and go home to Rhonda."

"No! I need to work. Stop trying to get rid of me." Brian pushed past Ray, and punched at the wall. "And stay away from my wife."

Brian fumed all the way to the elevator. He pushed the button four times in a row and paced. *Why won't it open?* He didn't want Ray to follow him. He didn't want to see Ray now, or ever again. Brian turned for the stairs right when the elevator door slid open. "Finally." The door closed and he breathed a sigh of relief.

When the car reached the third floor, Brian moved to step out.

Krissy ambled in.

He held her gaze and let the elevator door close. "What are you doing here?" Brian asked.

"Jake crank called me. I think it was him the entire time." She faced him and grinned, revealing a small dimple on the right corner of her mouth. "I came to see you."

"Look," Brian said. "I'm really sorry about the other day."

She shook her head. "No, I figured it out. Jake is seeing you as his therapist. It would be unethical and probably illegal for you to get mixed up with me."

"Still, I blew you off."

"No, you were being professional. I find that honorable." She took a step closer to him and her lilac spray lingered in his nostrils. "I was so desperate to get away from Jake that I used you."

Brian diverted his gaze.

"But I do like you, doctor." She ran her hand over his shoulder. "I'm just sorry things aren't different."

Brian tried to reject the voice in his head. Rhonda was awake and it was wrong to like another woman. But something in the recesses of his mind tempted him to follow his lust. On an impulse, Brian pushed the button to the basement and grabbed her in an ardent embrace.

❧

Ray searched for meaning behind the encounter with Brian.

Brian had actually tried to reach out to him and it had ended in disaster.

What just happened? He played the conversation back through his mind. It just didn't add up.

Every night for the past month, Rhonda would call, and then Ray would follow Brian home. His friend was always drunk when he arrived. Ray knew that he would have to do something soon to protect both Rhonda and the hospital.

Ray reached for the phone and dialed. It rang three times before Dr. Jai picked up.

"I think we have a serious problem."

❦

"Doc? Doc? Are you there, Doc?" Jake stood over Brian, who sat dazed in his chair. "Earth to the head hunter."

Brian blinked. Jake's face came into focus. "Jake?"

"Ah...we've made contact."

Brian sat up, rubbed at his face, and inhaled deeply. "When did you get here?"

"I've been standing here for the past five minutes, man. You OK? Need to talk?" Jake laughed.

"Very funny. I'm the doctor; you're the patient."

Jake laughed again. "Hard to tell right now, isn't it?"

Brian adjusted his tie and checked his watch. "OK, you have an hour. What do you want to talk about?"

"You, Doc. I want to talk about you."

Brian felt uneasy about his encounter with Krissy, and the last thing he wanted to talk about was himself. Especially now that he knew about Jake and Krissy's relationship. Brian shook his head. "That's not going to happen. Now, why don't we start with the murder you started to tell me about the other night."

Jake plopped down on the couch and placed his hands behind his neck. "Nah. I was thinking more about asking your daughter out. She's hot."

Brian came out of his chair. "Don't even think about it, Jake. You leave her alone."

Jake busted up laughing. "That was great, Doc. Oh, if only you could've seen your face."

"I don't have time for this. If you're going to tell jokes, then go do that at the halfway house," Brian said angrily.

"If I confess anything, you'll have to report me, right?"

"I do honor patient and doctor confidentiality, but if I'm called into court, then I have to testify to murder," Brian admitted. "So, yes."

Jake stood up and grabbed the Bible off the shelf.

"So, that's it, then. You're not going to talk?"

Jake plopped back down on the couch and opened the Book without answering.

Brian fumed. "What is wrong with you, huh?"

Jake looked up amused. "I must be crazy or I wouldn't be here, right?"

Brian stood and paced. "You come in here after hours ready to confess, and then you keep me here for another hour when I could have been at home."

"I thought you hated home."

Brian flinched. "I've never said that."

Jake shrugged and went back to his reading.

"You're missing the point," Brian said. "You didn't tell me a thing. Not really. I want to know, Jake, did you do it? Did you kill someone?"

Jake read for a minute before answering. "Yes and no."

Brian's shoulders felt heavy. He dropped back into the chair and covered his face with his hands. "You either did, or you didn't."

Jake swung his legs off the couch and faced Brian. "You're losing it, Doc. I don't think I'm the one who needs therapy."

"Did you do it?" Brian whispered.

Jake placed the Bible on the coffee table and leaned in. "Well, that's all in how you look at it."

"And how do *you* look at it, Jake?"

"From inside my head. You know, how I play out the memory. It feels like I killed her. But did I *really* do it? I'm not so sure."

"You're talking in riddles."

"Yes, I guess I am, Sam, I am."

"Maybe we should continue another day."

Jake stood and walked to the edge of Brian's desk. "I thought you liked spending time with me?"

"I do, Jake. I just don't have the patience for this. Things are a little stressful right now, and I don't feel like playing games with you."

"So, I'm getting to you. Is that it?"

Brian frowned. "Don't flatter yourself. You've just caught me on a bad day. I didn't get much sleep last night."

"More nightmares?"

Brian stared at Jake before responding. "How do you know about my nightmares?"

Jake laughed. "I don't. I just have them myself, so I assume that's what would keep a grown man from getting enough sleep."

Brian raised an eyebrow. "A grown man?"

"I may be younger than you, but I'm street smart. What I don't have in years, I make up for in experience."

Brian rolled his eyes.

"What? You don't believe me?"

"Never mind. Why don't you tell me something that you've read in the Bible?"

"Nice change of subject, Doc."

Brian moved back to the chair across from Jake. "For once, just answer the question."

"Fine." Jake stared at the Bible in his hand and said, "I only read one story."

"Really?" Brian asked lifting an eyebrow. "And what's that?"

"The story of David and Bathsheba."

"You mean to tell me that you spend hours at a time reading the same story over and over?"

"Yep."

"And why's that?"

Jake cracked his neck. "King David intrigues me."

"Why does he intrigue you?"

"Well, here's a guy who has been called a 'man after God's own heart,' and yet, he murdered a man to cover his own guilt."

Brian didn't read the Bible much, but he knew the story about David impregnating a married woman, Bathsheba, and then sending her husband to his death to cover his own sin.

"And why do you find that interesting?"

Jake gave a closed-mouth smile. "Because its nuts how far a man will go to cover up his own guilt."

Brian rounded his shoulders. "So, do you have anything you'd like to confess...without using a riddle?"

"Nah! It's not time. But don't worry. I won't murder a man to cover my crime." Jake winked.

"Jake, are you harassing Krissy Stephens?"

Jake's face went cold, his eyes narrowed. "You don't want to go there, Doc."

Brian swallowed. "Why not?"

Jake relaxed, apparently trying to mask his feelings. "You like her?"

Now Brian felt nauseous. "Don't be ridiculous. I'm a happily married man."

Jake crossed to Brian's desk and picked up his stress ball. "Married, yes. Happy, no."

"Look, Jake. I've told you. We have rules. We can only talk about you. Now answer the question. Are you harassing Ms. Stephens?"

Jake stared at the ball in his hands, watching the beads seep through his hands. "No, I'm not harassing her. We love each other." He looked at Brian with a heart-piercing look. "And you best write that down in your notes, Doc." He sat the ball back on the table. "Well, I think I'm done here for today. Don't you?"

"Yes, I think I've had..." Brian cleared his throat. "We've had enough. I'll see you next week."

"I look forward to it. You're the highlight of my week."

"The feeling is mutual, Jake. Now, I'll see you later."

Jake laughed and left.

A pain shot through Brian's abdomen. He grabbed his stomach and grimaced. Opening his desk drawer, he grabbed a roll of antacids and a bottle of scotch. He threw a couple nickel-sized chalks into his mouth, chewed, and washed it down with the golden spirits.

His heart sat in a pit of dejection. He missed his wife—her stunning smile, soft ivory skin, and lovely hair. Oh, how he missed loving her. It was getting difficult to remember their life together before the accident. No. He wouldn't think about that, couldn't think about that. Agony gripped his belly once more.

What was he doing with Krissy? He had no right to kiss her. It felt like an evil force drew him into her arms. Brian took another swig of his drink, and reached for his cell phone. Flipping it open, he dialed the familiar number.

The phone rang several times before he heard Rhonda say, "Hello?"

Brian opened his mouth, but some invisible force held his tongue.

"Hello?" she said again. "Brian, honey, is that you?"

Brian twisted the mouthpiece over his head and listened to her breathing. Water filled his eyes and he blinked to keep them from spilling over.

He hit the "cancel" button and the phone buzzed in his ear. Brian spotted the clock on the far wall. 3:00 PM. He had half-an-hour to his next appointment. He walked to the couch and lay down. His body ached. All the strain was taking its toll. He closed his eyes and within minutes, he slept.

15

"Welcome." The familiar, evil tone had returned.
Brian stared into the darkness, but saw nothing.
"Welcome to my world," said the voice again.
"Who are you?"
"All in good time," it hissed. "We have plenty of it."
Brian jolted awake, disoriented.

Someone knocked on the door.

"Come in," Brian said smoothing his hair.

"Excuse me, sir," Sheila said peeking around the door, "but Dr. Jai would like to have a word with you."

Brian nodded. He grabbed a tissue and wiped at his face. He adjusted his tie, and looked up to see the hospital board vice-president enter his office.

Brian stood. "Dr. Jai, so good to see you." He crossed the room to shake Dr. Jai's hand.

The serious Asian doctor nodded and motioned for Brian to sit on the couch.

Brian obeyed.

Dr. Jai sat behind Brian's desk, causing Brian to have to sit sideways to see him.

"Dr. Manifold, do you know why I'm here?"

"I assume because I missed the council meeting the other day."

"I wish that was the only reason, Doctor, but it's not." He folded his hands and placed them on Brian's desk. "You see, Doctor, my job is to make sure we have the best staff. Do you think you're the best staff?"

"Yes I do," Brian said.

"Hmm? I'm not so sure anymore." Dr. Jai stood and walked to the chair across from Brian, but didn't sit. "Do you know what I received on my desk this morning?"

No way did he want to know. Brian shook his head, but was sure his expression revealed his suspicion.

"I'm afraid it was a pretty disturbing report about your performance."

"Ray, jerk," Brian mumbled.

"I'm sorry? I didn't get that, Doctor. What did you say?"

"I just said that Ray...I mean, Dr. Jensen, is out to get me."

"On the contrary, Doctor. Jensen has been your best friend through this entire ordeal. He has defended you."

"Then who's reporting me?"

"Well now..." Dr. Jai encircled the chair and sat. "That would be the question, wouldn't it? But out of protection of those employees, I'm not at liberty to say."

"I see." Brian looked down at his hands.

"Do you?"

Brian met his stare. "I understand that someone doesn't want me here."

Dr. Jai raised an eyebrow. "So, it's a conspiracy, then?"

Brian shifted uncomfortably. "It must be. I'm a good doctor."

"Yes, I believe you are."

Brian shook his head. "I don't understand."

"You see, Dr. Manifold, you came to us with a

spotless record, and you've changed many lives during your tenure here. But a psychologist who doesn't know when to get help for himself can only hurt people. You realize you're at that point, don't you?"

"No, I don't. Why does everyone seem to think that I need help?" Brian asked. "I assure you. I'm fine."

Dr. Jai walked behind the couch where Brian sat. He placed his hand on Brian's left shoulder. "That's what I mean." He patted twice and started for the door. "I'll have Dr. Jensen book you an appointment to see someone outside our hospital next week." He turned back, his gaze stern. "That's not a recommendation, Dr. Manifold, but an order. Do I make myself clear?"

"Yes, sir."

Dr. Jai nodded and left.

Brian plummeted backward on the couch. Sweat seeped through his shirt. He rolled out of his jacket and dropped to the floor. *Can things get any worse?* Brian didn't want the answer to that question. He pressed his face into the forest green carpet and cried.

Am I losing my mind? Things at home were bad, but not at work. He needed his job. It kept him going. Maybe Dr. Jai was right. Maybe he needed to talk to someone. He needed to get out his frustration.

Brian inched along the floor toward the door. He used the knob to stand, and then shut and locked the door. He went to his desk and pulled a flask from inside the drawer. His hand shook as he brought the bottle to his mouth. Instantly, the drink soothed him.

Who am I kidding? I'm just fine. Everyone else needs to get a grip. He wiped his eyes and rang his secretary.

"Sheila, is my last appointment here yet?"

"No, sir," she said. "They've canceled."

"Good," he said. "Go home. I'll see you tomorrow."

"Yes, sir."

Brian shut off his banker's lamp and stood in the darkness. His stomach churned. Maybe he needed to see a medical doctor; his stomach had bothered him for months.

Brian pushed another mouthful of bourbon back in his throat and swallowed. He didn't want to go home, but he also didn't want to stay here. Where could he go? He peeked out the blinds.

Cars raced by at a maddening pace, and in a polarized fashion, boats sailed in the distance without a care.

It was late fall. The beaches were probably deserted. He took another drink, snapped off his light, and headed out. He would go to the beach.

The elevator door opened and Ray walked out.

"Hi, Brian."

Brian stepped into the elevator without a word and pushed to close the door.

"Brian, don't be like that. Come on, I came down to talk to you." Ray stepped back into the elevator.

Brian shook his head and pushed the "open" button.

"I'll take the next one," Brian said and stepped back out.

"Brian…"

Brian waved to the closing door.

⁂

Ray pushed the button to the lower floor. When the door opened, he stepped out into the parking garage, saw a familiar face, and smiled. "Going home?"

Danielle turned from her car door. "Yes, it's been a long day."

He walked around his car next to her. "I would agree with you there."

"Any change with the Brian situation?"

"No," he said simply.

"I'm sorry."

Her blue eyes sparkled in the florescent light. She really was a beautiful woman. The pull that drew him earlier beckoned him again.

The elevator opened, and a few employees filtered out. He waited for them to dissipate to their own cars, cleared his throat and looked at her. "Are you free right now?" he asked.

"Yes." She grinned.

"How about we get something to eat. I'm starved."

"I'd love that." She slammed her door closed and hit the alarm. It beeped, echoing in the garage. "You driving?"

"Apparently." He laughed. "Come on."

They walked to his sedan, and he let her in the passenger door. As he walked around the back of the car, his stomach flipped in anticipation. He felt like a young boy going on his first date. Why did this girl bring that out in him? Never had he felt so comfortable and so out-of-sorts at the same time. It was exhilarating.

He climbed in and started the engine. Jazz music blared through the speakers. He turned down the knob volume and offered an embarrassed smile. "Sorry."

She giggled. "Perfectly fine. I like mine loud, too."

"What kind of music do you listen to?" he asked,

as he pulled the car out of the garage and onto the street.

"I'm kind of eclectic. Mostly eighties new wave, though R&B, rock, basically anything without twang works for me."

"Anything but twang?" he repeated, amused.

"I don't really care for country. Guess I'm a city girl through-and-through."

"I don't know if we can be friends, then."

Her eyes grew wide. "Seriously?"

He laughed. "My mom is a huge country gospel fan. She may not approve."

Danielle stared, and then nodded. "I see, so you're a mama's boy."

Inside, Ray cringed. He'd heard that joke so many times. But he knew she was joking, so he pretended to check his mirror before responding. "Do you like Japanese food?"

"Love it."

"Then how about we eat at Wasabi Grill? It's only a few blocks from here."

"Sounds wonderful."

A few minutes later, they parked in the lot and he let her out. A cool breeze blew up from the ocean a few yards away.

Danielle pulled her arms around her, shivering.

"You cold?" he asked.

"A little."

He pulled his jacket off and placed it around her shoulders.

"Thanks."

"Sure." He escorted her inside.

The restaurant was glass on three sides, two of them overlooking the water. The host walked them to a back table in the corner and offered them large black menus.

"Thanks."

"Would you like anything to drink?"

Ray looked at Danielle.

"I'd like hot green tea, please," she said.

Ray nodded. "The same."

The host walked away, and Ray laid down his menu to stare at his gorgeous date.

Her gaze searched the pictures of fish and rice. "What do you recommend?" she asked, not looking up.

"I usually get a Philadelphia roll."

Her finger slid across the page, landing on the picture. "Salmon, avocado, cucumber and cream cheese." She smiled and closed her menu. "Sold. Anything with cream cheese is a good idea."

He laughed. "Haven't you had sushi before?"

"Oh sure, if you count California rolls and ebi shrimp."

"Nope, I guess not." He smiled.

Their gazes locked.

He wished he knew what she was thinking. Did she feel the same magnetic force? She said she wanted to be more than friends. Maybe he needed to have that defined. He leaned forward.

Slowly, her face moved towards his.

Adrenaline coursed through his system. Their lips lay millimeters apart, her breath warm on his face. He closed his eyes, longing to touch his lips to hers.

"I ready take order."

Ray pulled his gaze from her and looked to their Asian waiter, disappointed. "We'll both have a couple Philadelphia rolls, two orders of ebi shrimp, a

California roll, ginger salads and some onion soup."

The man bowed, gathered the menus, and left them alone.

Ray glanced back at Danielle. "You take my breath away."

"I wasn't sure you'd want to start anything right now."

He sat back, placing his napkin on his lap. "And why is that?"

She diverted her stare to the table.

He knew the answer that would alter everything. "Things are tough, but they'll get better."

"Can you talk about it?"

"Not really." Though Brian wasn't his patient, still, confidentiality was huge in their environment. *And in our friendship.* "What I can say is the man needs prayer. Lots of it."

"I sensed that." She bit her lip and sighed. "You want to change the subject?"

"Without a doubt." He smiled. "Let's talk about you."

"Me?"

His gaze filtered over her manicured hands and up to her face. A small freckle kissed the side of her temple. Secretly, he wanted to touch it. This woman had some spell over him. It empowered him, and for once, he wasn't frightened. "What do you want to be when you grow up? Besides working as an assistant."

"Hmm, aren't I grown up, now?" She grinned.

"Debatable." He winked, clearly kidding.

She playfully punched his arm. "Let's see, I'm twenty-six. I guess to you I'm still a baby."

Wow, they were eleven years apart. He'd never realized that. Was that OK? He studied her expression.

He didn't care if she didn't. "Well, when I grow up, I plan to sit around and paint."

She raised an eyebrow. "Paint? You?"

He shrugged. "It's a hobby I used to have in college. As I started working, I never had time anymore. But I miss it."

"I'd love to see some of your paintings, sometime."

The waiter brought three orange, boat-shaped bowls filled with sushi. Another waiter stepped behind him with bowls of soup and salad. The two men bowed and left them to eat.

Ray picked up his chopsticks and started rubbing them together to get rid of any splinters. "If I can find any of my paintings, I'll let you see them."

"I bet your mother has them displayed somewhere important." Danielle smiled and unfolded her napkin into her lap.

A painting of a purple horse was prominently displayed over his mother's sewing table. Not exactly art he wanted to show Danielle. "Well, I don't know if it counts. My mom has stuff from grade school out in the open."

"I can't wait to meet her," Danielle said, with a twinkle in her eye.

"Yeah, I bet." Ray folded his two sticks around the round rice disc, and dipped it in soy sauce. "That's because you don't know her."

"My parents passed away when I was a teenager. I envy people who have folks."

"I'm sorry."

"It was years ago." She poured more soy sauce into a small dish by her plate. "This is really good."

"It is. So, tell me about your hobbies. What do you

like to do when you aren't dealing with doctors like me?"

She swallowed the bite in her mouth, and then took a sip of tea. "I'm not really an artsy person at all, but I enjoy reading. I read everything. Romances, suspense thrillers, poetry, autobiographies—"

"What are you reading right now?" Ray asked.

"Hmm..." She pinched her lips together, obviously thinking. "I think the last thing I read was..." she named a book by a famous author.

He stared at her, amazed. This woman was nothing like he originally imagined. She was intelligent, interesting, and claiming his heart. "That's deep. Did you like it?"

"Yeah, there are so many layers to it. I like writings like that. I want to think, you know?" She smiled. "I guess if I could change professions, I'd teach literature."

"Not a doctor?"

She laughed. "We'll see what God wants for me." She popped a green chunk of wasabi in her mouth and started fanning at her mouth. "Hot!" She glanced around the table, obviously in search of water.

"Hold on." Ray jumped up and ran to the counter. "Can I get a glass of water, no ice, for my date?"

The woman nodded.

Ray glanced back at Danielle. Her eyes were red and tearing.

"Here you go," the woman said, handing him a glass of water.

"Thank you." Ray rushed it to Danielle.

She guzzled it down within seconds, and then looked at him, embarrassed. "That was dumb, huh?"

"I'm sorry, I didn't realize."

"I'll live." She held up a hand, and laughed. "Well, once I can feel my tongue again, that is."

Still laughing, he tossed enough money on the table to cover the check and a generous tip. He glanced up at Danielle. "Are you ready to go?"

She laughed. "Oh, yeah."

16

A blanket of fog covered the beach. Only a few surfers could be seen in the water.

Brian loosened his tie and removed his shoes and socks. He placed his feet in the supple earth and let the soft crystals seep between his toes. The sand was cold but soothing on his feet. He sat and looked out across the waves. Tall walls of water beat hard against the shore. A few seagulls combed the beach.

Brian breathed the salty air deep into his lungs, closed his eyes and lay back on the malleable surface. The rhythmic sound of the ocean crashing—in and out—soon lulled him to sleep.

ॐॐ

"I was right, wasn't I?"

Brian opened his eyes. *Where am I?*

Except for the moon above, darkness surrounded him. Brian strained to see the backdrop. It appeared to be a field of some sort. Black feather-like trees swayed in the distance, a soft, chilling wind blew against his bare arms. He stepped forward and his feet squished in ground muddied by the moisture in the air.

"I was right, wasn't I?" came the voice again.

"About what?" Brian bellowed.

"You're not going to make it."

Brian stood ready for the beast this time. "I'm just

fine," he said, through clenched teeth. "Do you hear me? I'm fine!"

A shadow appeared from behind a tree. It didn't come close enough for Brian to see its horrid face, but he sensed it was the monster from before.

"No, Brian, you're not. You're nothing more than a forlorn, futile human being."

"This isn't real. This whole field is some sick nightmare. When I open my eyes, I'll be back in my bed. So, I know I'm OK."

The beast laughed a vile cackle that iced Brian's blood to the core. "Don't you know where you are?"

"No."

"Where is reality, Brian? Where does your world end and my world begin?"

Brian thought about that. "I suppose in my dreams."

"Very good." It hissed. "But which world is real?"

"The one where I'm comfortably sleeping in my bed at home. And you...you're no more than a fabrication shaped by the results of a temporary psychosis brought on by a bad experience."

The creature stepped out from behind the shadow. Puss oozed from its eyes and foam dripped from its mouth.

Brian swallowed against the bile that rose in his throat.

"I'm more real than you can imagine. The sooner you believe in me, the sooner you can deal with the things in your so-called reality." The beast scratched Brian's arm with a talon.

He screamed. It burned like acid on his skin, revealing a small welt with effervescent pus. "So, you really exist?" Brian nursed his arm, and much to his relief, it stepped back into the darkness.

"What's real to you will soon surprise you."

Brian inched closer to the dark shadow. "I'm sick of riddles. I want facts. Just spell it out for me and be done with it."

"I'm sorry," hissed the beast. "But I can't do that. No one can, but you."

"Another riddle?"

Silence. Only the gentle hum of the wind caressing the trees could be heard. Brian strained to see the creature, but it was gone. He collapsed to the wet grass and shut his eyes. He tried to block the beast's words from his mind, but they ate at him.

What is real to you will soon surprise you.

ॐॐ

Cold, Brian opened his eyes. The sun sank below the horizon and cast purple and orange ripples along the skyline.

Brian stretched, and remembered his dream. He felt his arm and sighed. It was only a dream. He looked at his watch. *Wow. I was asleep for almost two hours.* He dusted the sand from his suit and returned to his car.

The voice from his nightmare cycled through his mind. Because of his professional background, Brian didn't just throw dreams away as pure nonsense. Often, dreams were a window into a person's masked anguish, among other things.

But this persistent creature disturbed him. *What's he trying to tell me?* He would have to analyze it later. Maybe when he hadn't been drinking.

Of course, Brian didn't know when that would be. Nowadays he seemed to always need a nip. He stretched and popped his neck. He would figure it out later. He had enough stress in his life. For now, he would grab a bite to eat and visit a bar.

⌘

Danielle smiled as she and Ray left the restaurant. Outside, the sun had set. The waves could only be heard in the dark distance.

Ray reached to open his door, but something stopped him. Or rather, someone. He started to cross the street, but a car started and pulled out of the lot. He jumped into the driver's seat and started the engine. His cell rang.

"Ray speaking." His car glided out of the lot, in pursuit of the vehicle. "Yeah, I'm behind him. Don't worry, I'll follow him home." He stopped at a red light, but the other car didn't. "Shoot!" Ray hit the steering wheel. "No, I promise. Bye." The light turned green. He gunned it.

Danielle's pulse hammered in her ears as the car raced through a yellow light. "Is everything OK?"

"We need to take a slight detour."

The car ahead turned left.

Ray did the same.

"It's Brian, isn't it?"

Ray glanced at her, but didn't answer.

They rode in stressed silence the rest of the way.

Danielle didn't understand the madness. Why didn't Ray just call the police?

Brian was clearly driving drunk. He needed to be arrested.

But she feared voicing her opinion.

This was obviously something Ray felt very

passionate about.

But was it right to be silent, either? When they stopped, she'd try to broach the subject.

The car ahead swerved, almost hitting a parked car.

Danielle gasped.

"Only two more blocks," Ray muttered under his breath.

Finally, the car rolled over the curb, and into a driveway.

Ray parked a safe distance away and shut off his lights.

They watched as Brian climbed out his car, stumbled up the walk and into the house.

Ray exhaled. "Ready?"

"Why do you do that?"

Ray scrunched his eyebrows. "Do what?"

"Help him like that? Why don't you call the authorities?" She waved her hands to the house. "He is going to kill someone if you don't turn him in."

"That's why I follow him home. To make sure—"

"You can't protect anyone a block behind. What if someone was to run out into the street? What if a mother with a van full of kids was to come around the corner at the wrong time?" Her voice rose. "What if a—"

"I'm not going to turn in my friend." His jaws clenched.

"Even if it makes you an accessory to murder?"

Ray stared out at the road, his knuckles white on the steering wheel.

The tension in the car hung heavy.

Maybe she'd gone too far. It wasn't her intention to hurt him. She just wanted him to see the danger he was playing with. She opened her mouth to speak, and then snapped it closed. What was there to say? Truthfully, she knew she was right.

"I promised," he whispered.

She peered sideways at him. "Promised what?"

"To take care of him." Ray faced her, and tears were visible in his eyes.

Her heart softened. "Letting him drive around drunk isn't saving him. It'll get him killed."

He stared at her moment, took a huge breath, and then started the engine.

It was obvious the discussion was over, and that their perfect night had ended badly.

What she wouldn't do to go back to when they'd almost kissed.

❧

Brian quietly shut the door to his house and stumbled toward his bedroom. The light flipped on from under the door, and he stopped short. He put his hand to his mouth and blew. His breath reeked of alcohol. If Rhonda was awake, she'd be furious. Brian patted his pockets for some gum, to no avail. He tiptoed past their bedroom door, to the kitchen, and opened the refrigerator door.

"Brian?"

Brian took a deep breath and peeked over the top of the door. "Hi, honey," he said with mock cheerfulness. "Glad to see you're awake."

"Where have you been?" she asked. "It's one o'clock in the morning, and you promised to come home and talk."

"Oh, sorry," he said, ducking in search of a smelly

food. "I had a rough day and went for a drive to clear my head. Time must have got away from me." Brian spotted some string cheese. He ripped open the package and stuffed it in his mouth.

"Brian, have you been drinking?"

Brian coughed. The cheese lodged in his throat. His eyes watered as he worked to swallow it.

Rhonda watched with arms crossed, not amused.

"Hey, just a little one to unwind. What's the big deal?" Brian slammed the door closed and traversed to the living room with Rhonda at his heels.

"We need to talk about your drinking, Brian. It's out of control."

"Stop it!" Brian faced her. "I'm fine. Got it?"

"No, Brian. You're a drunk."

Heat slammed into Brian's skull. "I think I liked you better catatonic."

Rhonda's lip trembled and a tear grazed her cheek. She nodded. Without another word, she walked back to their room and slammed the door.

"Rhonda, I'm sorry," he squeaked.

The light under the door snapped off.

He felt horrible. He'd wanted his wife back in his life and look at the way he treated her. But she deserved it, didn't she? After all, Brian had enough people telling him to change. He didn't need anyone in his family singing the same song. He needed her to support him.

Ray probably got to her. *Ray*. His very name made Brian's blood sear. Yes, they were best friends at one time, but when he opted to take a management job—a job that made Ray Brian's supervisor, things changed. Sure, Brian was jealous at first, but he'd still been happy for his friend. Until Ray turned into super jerk.

⤳⤳

Ray walked Danielle to the door, but didn't wait around for any goodnight kiss. He was still angry with her. Maybe even a little angry with himself. Deep down, he knew she was right. But he was fixing this.

Brian was on the verge of getting help. Everything would be OK.

If Danielle couldn't support him in that, then she wasn't the woman for him.

He drove into the carport and climbed out of his car. A deep depression washed over him. How long had he endured this battle with his friend? The physical toll of little sleep and worry was beginning to age him. As he unlocked the door, he began to pray. "Jesus, I need You more than ever. Am I doing the right thing? I don't think I can do this much longer."

He dropped his keys in a bowl by the door and walked to the kitchen. A plate of brownies sat in the middle of the table. His mother had been by. Most likely, they were fat-free or made out of something healthy and tasteless.

Ray dropped to the couch, kicked off his shoes, and then flipped on the TV. Light filled the dark space. Black and white images flashed on the screen. He hadn't seen this movie since he was a kid. He turned up the volume, and allowed the fantasy world to take over his mind. No longer did he want to think about Brian. Or Danielle, for that matter. He just wanted to feel peace.

But no matter how much he tried to be engrossed in the story, the TV characters just made him more miserable. Apparently, no amount of peace would come from their sad story. He shut it off, and switched on the light. His Bible caught his eye. Part of him wanted to ignore it and go to bed. But a pastor once told him, "If you don't feel like doing something with the Lord, that's probably when you need it the most."

Reluctantly, Ray reached for the black Book and flipped it open to Psalms. The peace chapter, his mother once called it. He scanned the page, his eyes falling on 31:24. *Be strong and take heart, all you who hope in the LORD.*

Tears formed and grazed his cheek. Ray didn't bother to wipe them away. The Lord knew his pain, and thought enough to show him this verse. *Thank you, Lord. I will not give up on Brian. You haven't.*

❧❧

Brian opened his eyes. Light filtered through the blinds. He must have fallen asleep on the couch in his suit.

"Good morning, Dad." Lara sat across from him, nursing a glass of orange juice.

"What time is it?"

"Around eight in the morning."

Brian jumped up. "Oh, no! Why didn't you wake me?"

"You looked tired."

"Great. I'm going to be late again." Brian ran to his room.

Rhonda lay motionless on the bed.

He shook his head and grabbed a fresh suit. Skipping the shower, he pulled off his clothes from the night before and stepped into the new ones.

"Rhonda?"

She didn't stir.

"Well, I see things are back to normal." He fixed his tie, and ran a comb through his hair. "I'll be home late." He grabbed his briefcase and headed out.

"Hey, Dad," Lara said from behind him.

Brian turned around. "Yes?"

"Don't forget to come to Parents' Night tomorrow night. It's very important to me that you come."

"I'll be there. You can count on it," he said and closed the door.

17

Ray parked in front of his childhood home and shut off the engine. His mom had called that morning in desperate need of her prescription. Her car wouldn't start, so Ray, as always, came to her rescue. He walked up the cobblestone path and knocked on the door.

"Come in, Ray."

He wiped his feet on the rust-colored mat and pushed the door open.

His mother lay in her brown chair with an ice bag on her head, eyes closed, most likely for dramatic effect.

"Hi, Mom," Ray said.

She pulled the bag into her lap and stuck out her cheek.

Ray crossed to her chair and kissed her. "You're not feeling well?"

"I should have taken my insulin hours ago. My blood sugars are out of control."

His mother did a lot of things for attention and this was no exception. But she did struggle with diabetes.

Ray dug in the white bag and pulled out a glass vial. "Where is your syringe?"

She pointed to the kitchen. "Top drawer next to the stove."

He handed her the medicine and went in search of a syringe.

"Do you remember my neighbor, Elizabeth Fox?" His mother yelled from the other room.

"Not really." The drawer by the stove was filled with many things—a mousetrap, a calculator, a thermometer, at least three can openers, needle and thread, a dozen or so pizza coupons, recipe cards—but he didn't see a syringe. "Mom, it's not here."

"You're not looking."

He pushed the junk around again. "I'm looking, Mom. It's not here."

She huffed. "Why do I bother to ask?"

Good question. He stepped out of the way to let her near the drawer.

She pushed the stuff around, and produced a syringe.

He raised an eyebrow. "It wasn't there a minute ago."

"Uh huh." She frowned and went to work on giving herself the medication. "So, are you sure you don't remember my neighbor? She used to babysit you when you were young."

No bells were ringing. "Sorry, no."

His mother tossed the syringe on the counter and took a seat at the table. "Well, you should. Anyways, she has a niece named—"

"No, Mom. I didn't come here to be introduced to a girl."

The front door opened.

"Aah, there she is now."

No way. Ray's eyes went wide. "Mother," he hissed.

She smiled, pretending to ignore him. "We're in here, Tori."

This was not good. *Think of a way out.* He glanced

around the kitchen, not that there was a back door in this place. How could his mom do this to him? She'd tricked him. Probably had an entire stash of insulin in her closet. "Does your car work, Mom?"

"Never been better." She stood and winked at the brunette who walked in the door. "Tori, I'm so glad you could come. This is my son, Ray. Ray, Tori. She's in marketing."

Ray smiled uncomfortably. "Nice to meet you."

She grinned. "You, too. Your mom tells me you're a psychologist?"

"Psychiatrist. Yes." He stuffed his hands in his pockets and rocked on his heels. How could he get out of here gracefully?

"Well, you'll have to ignore my son. He's a bit shy around the ladies."

"Mom!" This was unacceptable.

"I'm making this easy for you. Tori and I already discussed it, and she'd love to go out with you this Friday night."

Unbelievable! He shook his head. "You are—" Words could not explain how angry he was at this moment. "I'm sorry, Tori. I'm sure you're an amazing woman, but I'm sort of seeing someone."

His mother laughed.

"You know what, Mom, I love you, but don't call me for a while." Ray started for the door.

"Raymond. Sweetheart. Come back."

He didn't stop. Why couldn't she just let him be? Even if things with Danielle didn't work out, it was *his* love life. He ducked into his car and cranked up the music. He needed to get to work, anyway.

Brian would be there soon.

❧

Brian screeched into his parking space, leaving tread in his path. He bounded from the car, snatched his briefcase, and double-timed up the stairs. When he reached the top of the staircase, he peeked around the door. All clear. He bolted for his office.

"Good morning, Dr. Manifold," Sheila said, stepping out of his office door.

"Sheila? What are you doing in my office?" Brian asked, out of breath.

"I let Dr. Richards in," she said.

"You mean he's in there?" Brian pointed to his door, sickened. Dr. Richards was Dr. Jai's personal assistant.

She nodded slowly, a grin forming on her face.

What is she smiling about? Brian looked at his watch. "Well, did you cover for me?"

She shook her head.

"That's just great, Sheila. Now, I'm in trouble."

Sheila shrugged and returned to her desk.

Brian stared at the door. It felt like the entrance to purgatory. *Big breath.* He squared his shoulders and marched in with mock confidence.

"Dr. Manifold? So nice of you to join us," Dr. Richards said.

Brian set his briefcase on the desk and turned to face the older man. "Yes, I overslept."

"I see. Well, when you're plenty rested, Dr. Jai would like a word with you."

"Yes, sir."

❧

Brian sat awkwardly across from Dr. Jai. The man

hadn't talked in over five minutes. Brian looked at the exit, longing to run out.

"Do you have somewhere to be?" Dr. Jai asked, finally.

"As a matter of fact, I do have an appointment at ten," Brian said.

Dr. Jai slapped his hand on his desk and stood. He was a short man, but wielded a power of intimidation better than a person twice his size. "Dr. Manifold, what am I going to do with you? I like you. I always have, but the more I read in this report," he said, pointing to a blue folder on his desk, "the more I dread your future."

"Are you firing me?" Brian blurted.

Dr. Jai let out a soft chuckle. "Well, it would seem the right decision, but I haven't made one yet. I need to think about it some more. The board convenes in a couple more days. I will let them decide."

"Can I see the report?" Brian asked.

Dr. Jai pressed his lips together and glanced back at the folder. "I don't know."

"I do have the right to defend myself, do I not? Are you taking everybody's word as truth without ever asking me my side of things?"

"The number one complaint is that you're never on time. Do you deny that, Dr. Manifold?"

Brian looked down at his hands. "No." He obviously couldn't deny that charge.

"The second is that you drink on the job. Do you deny that?"

"What?" Brian furrowed his eyebrows. "I would never even think about such an act."

Dr. Jai walked around his desk and pulled a familiar leather flask out of his drawer. "This isn't mine, doctor. Would you like to reverse your plea?"

"Where did you get that?" Brian asked, incriminating himself more with every syllable.

"Do you really need to ask that?"

"Dr. Richards?"

"Yes."

Brian slumped in his chair, wanting to disappear. "May I ask who reported me?"

"I won't feed you specific names for vengeance, Doctor. But I will tell you that everyone on your floor has concurred with the opinion of the report."

"Everyone?" Brian's mind flashed to Danielle and Sheila.

"Yes, everyone."

Brian's temples pulsed. He didn't speak; he only looked at his hands. "You told me to go to therapy. I thought that was going to be enough."

"I hadn't finished reading the report when I ordered you to go, but we'll see." He stood. "It is almost ten. I have an appointment, too. So, if you'll excuse me."

"Yes, sir."

"I think under the circumstances, Doctor, you might want to go home for the day."

"Yes, sir." Dejected, Brian stood and trudged back to his floor. How could Danielle and Sheila turn on him? Especially Danielle.

He buzzed Sheila.

"Yes, sir?"

"You're done for the day. Go home."

"It's only ten."

Brian set the phone back in its cradle and extended his arms. He was vanquished. He needed a drink.

⊱⊰

Ray picked up the phone and dialed the Manifold house.

Rhonda answered on the first ring.

"Rhonda? This is Ray. Is Brian there?"

"No, I thought he was at work."

"He left around ten." Ray looked at the clock on the wall. It read 5:00 PM. "Do you have any idea where he would go?"

"What's going on, Ray?"

"He had a pretty bad day, and I want to make sure he's OK. Do you know where he might be?"

"You have to ask?"

"Understood," he said, and then added, "Look, I'll find him and call you later."

"Thank you, Ray. I don't know what I would do without you."

⊱⊰

Brian sat at *Wally's Watering Hole*. He was joined by a Vietnam vet who proudly conveyed over a dozen village stories before Brian was drunk. He hardly heard the vet's final story. Brian's mind was focused on the amber liquid he held in his hand.

Wally had just declared it his last.

In reverent ceremony, Brian brought the glass to his lips, pushed the drink down his throat and swallowed. His head swam in a sea of colors. "Are you sure I can't have another?" Brian asked the heavy muscle behind the counter.

"Goodnight, Brian," the bartender said. "I'll see you tomorrow."

Brian nodded like a bobble-head doll and plummeted off his stool.

Wally looked over the bar while wiping a glass with a rag. "You OK, man?"

"Yeah, I'll be fine," Brian said and pushed up. "I've got another bottle in my pocket."

"Do yourself a favor. Go home and sleep it off."

"What are you, my mother? Do yourself a favor and don't tell me what to do, Wally." Brian pulled a brown paper bag from his pocket, and held it up high. "There is one thing left in my life that I can control and that is how much I drink."

Wally came around from behind the counter and helped Brian to the door. "No, man. I think the drink controls you."

Brian stepped back and took a swing at Wally's head. He hit air and fell at the bartender's feet.

"Come on, man. Don't start being a mean drunk. I won't be able to let you back in my bar again." Wally led Brian out the door.

"That's fine," Brian spat. "Cause there's twenty more on this block alone."

"All right, Brian. Sit here," Wally said, setting Brian down on a bus stop bench just outside. "Take the bus. Don't even think about driving home. OK?"

"Yeah, sure."

Wally shook his head and entered the dim building.

Brian peered down the block. The streets were wet and empty. A single amber light marked the yellow condo door in the distance. Krissy. He wanted to see her. A friend. He needed a friend. He stood up, but then sat back down. *What am I thinking?* He stared at the yellow door. It was like a beacon in the water.

She was probably in there alone, crying about losing Jake.

He had to comfort her. After all, he was her doctor. He stood back up, head swimming. He stepped into the street just in time to dodge a beat up pickup truck.

That was close! What am I doing?

He pushed back up and swaggered to the door. Leaning against the door jamb, he rapped with the back of his hand.

Nothing.

He lifted his hand to knock again when he heard the knob turn.

"Can I help you?" an elderly Hispanic man said from behind the chained door.

Brian blinked to focus. "I'm looking for Krissy Stephens."

"No Krissy lives here," he said and closed the door.

Brian looked around.

The yellow door was the only one that faced the street.

He was sure that she had said she lived there.

Confused, Brian moved back to the bus stop and his view of the yellow door.

18

Ray drove futilely for hours. He'd stopped at almost every bar around their neighborhood and had decided to give up, when he remembered Brian's fascination with San Diego's Gaslamp district.

Finally, around midnight, Ray spotted Brian at a bus stop nursing a bottle in a brown paper bag. Ray pulled his car to the curb and got out.

Brian glanced up, but quickly looked away.

Ray eased himself onto the seat next to Brian.

"Ah, my best friend. Come to pour salt in my wound?"

"Do you see yourself?" Ray asked. "You're one step away from skid row, my friend."

"Is that how you start with all your patients? If so, I hope they get their money back."

"You're not my patient, Brian. You're my colleague. And you *need* help."

"I'm fine," Brian slurred. "I'm just having a little nightcap before I have to go home and face the stiff in my bed."

Ray stared at Brian. "You and Rhonda need to talk. Look at what this mess has done to you."

"I'm fine. Just fine."

"No, you're not *fine!* Stop saying you're *fine!* You're anything but *fine!*" Ray took a breath to calm himself. "The guilt of your past is killing you. You either talk this out or you're going to hit rock bottom."

Brian toasted the air and laughed cynically. "Already there, my friend. Already there."

"So, you admit you need help?"

"No, I agree I've hit rock bottom." Brian took another swig from the bottle. "I'm all alone in this world now, and thanks to you, the one thing I had left is gone, too." Brian wiped his face.

"Thanks to me?" Ray wrapped his arm around the back of the bench.

"You and that stupid report. Now everyone is trying to bury me."

"Who's trying to bury you?"

"All the people I trusted the most." He glared at Ray. "Especially you." Brian took another drink. "Not that I've trusted you for quite some time."

Ray placed his hand on Brian's shoulder. "I'm here to help you. I know you don't believe that, but it couldn't be more true."

Brian flung Ray's hand off. "I don't need your help! What I need is my life back to the way it was."

"Let's talk about your daughter, Brian."

Brian fell off the seat and hit his head against a metal trashcan.

Ray caught his breath.

Unfazed, Brian pushed himself up. "You leave her out of this."

Ray reached a hand down to Brian, but he batted it away. "Look, Brian, you need to talk about what happened."

"No, I don't. The only thing I have to do is take care of *me*. Now, if you'll excuse me, I need to get home." Brian stumbled toward his vehicle.

Ray's heart felt heavy. He reached out and firmly grasped Brian's arm. "I can't let you drive home."

Brian spat on the sidewalk, just missing Ray's designer oxford shoes. "You can't stop me, Ray."

"I will, if you make me. Now, give me your keys."

"No!" Brian jammed his hands into his pockets and looked away.

"Please." Ray pleaded. "Don't do this."

"Why not?"

Ray forced Brian to look him in the eye. "Because bad things happen when you drink."

Brian stared at Ray for a moment, and then buckled to the ground sobbing.

Ray couldn't hold back any longer. He knelt by his broken friend and allowed the tears to flow.

Brian wept bitterly for a good five minutes.

Ray held his friend and prayed for a miracle.

Finally, Brian seemed to calm down.

Ray helped him to his feet. "Come on, I'll drive you home."

⮞⮜

"Have you figured it out yet?" hissed the beast.

Brian blinked. He lay on the floor of his living room floor covered in blood. Brian looked around the house. The darkness made it hard to see clearly. He rubbed his body for wounds, but found none.

"Have you figured it out yet?"

Brian stood. Blood poured from his hands. His face went white. He grabbed the afghan on the couch to stop the blood. He stubbed his toe on the coffee table and cursed aloud.

"You'll never make it."

Brian groaned. "Stop playing with me. Tell me what you want."

The creature laughed. "It isn't what I *want*. It's what controls you that draws me. Your sin has all the power."

"My sin?"

"Do you deny your part in this story?"

"What story?" Brian staggered through the house like a blind man. He couldn't remember his place being this dark before. He felt hot air on the back of his neck and the sound of deep breathing. Brian turned his head slowly to the right and found his face only inches from the beast's mouth. Brian's stomach churned as the dragon-like face opened. He squeezed his eyes shut, ready to be swallowed. "Please, just leave me alone," Brian pleaded.

"I'm afraid that isn't possible. You've given me reign, and I rather enjoy it."

Brian opened his eyes.

The beast licked its razor-sharp fangs and smiled an eerie grin. "We'll be spending lots of time together."

"What are you?"

"A smart doctor, like you. I thought you would have figured that out by now."

Brian wiped perspiration from his face.

The creature circled Brian, its talons grating his clothes. "I'm an evil spirit. A demon."

Brian stepped back. "You're merely a mirage. A nauseating dream. Satan is only a myth."

The creature inched closer. "I'm more genuine than most other things in your life."

"I don't believe in you." Brian continued to back up, his heart pulsating through his ribs. He placed his hands behind his back to make sure he didn't run into anything.

"What's to believe in, Brian? Belief is what you

see."

"No! Faith is things unseen, and I don't believe in you. You're only a nightmare."

The demon reached out his long claw, almost scratching Brian's face. "No, you pathetic little man. I'm indisputably, genuinely, unadulterated, without a doubt—*REAL.*"

19

Danielle opened her eyes. Her heart raced, but the light from the street eased her mind. She glanced at the clock by her bed. 4:00 AM. Something stirred her spirit again. The need to pray overwhelmed her. But for whom?

She tried to roll over and go back to sleep, but Holy Spirit would not let her. Silently she prayed for an hour. When she finally felt a sense of peace, she got up, showered and dressed for work. It was still an hour before she usually went in, but what else did she have to do? *I'll get coffee on the way.*

Danielle opened the outside door and breathed deep. The early morning air felt intoxicating. She closed the door.

In the distance, a small shaft of light marked the horizon.

Anticipation of a new day. She hoped that included Ray. Making him mad was not what she wanted. Maybe her advice wasn't what he needed. Right or wrong, he'd counted on her being a friend. She sighed, silently praying for another chance.

Traffic was sparse, and Danielle made it to work in record time. She parked, and then noticed one other car. Dr. Manifold's. A part of her wanted to turn around and go home. To be in the office with only him seemed like a bad plan.

Someone knocked on her window and she

jumped.

Bernie stood outside with his hands on his hips.

Danielle opened the door and stepped out. "Good morning, Bernie."

"Here a little early, miss?"

She nodded and popped her trunk. "Couldn't sleep."

"Well, you'll have to go around through emergency. I have my orders to keep the main door closed for another hour."

Danielle stared at the guard. His military posture clearly said he wasn't kidding. "Fine. Thanks for your help."

Bernie nodded and retreated to his booth.

Having Bernie here made her a little more at ease. Danielle headed to the ER, and cut over to her side of the building. The halls were eerie quiet, and many of the lights were still off. She flipped them on as she walked. Her heart pulsed. As she approached Brian's door, she thought about going in and talking to him. Maybe if she was able to turn him around, Ray would forgive her.

She reached for the knob, but heard Brian say something. He wasn't alone.

ॐॐ

Brian tossed back a glass of bourbon, before turning to address his daughter.

"Lara," Brian said. "What are you doing here? Shouldn't you be on your way to school?"

Lara hugged him. "I wanted to remind you about the function at my school tonight."

Brian had forgotten. He nodded. "Yes, yes, of

course. I'll be there."

"Dad, can we talk?"

Brian gave her a weak smile and pointed to the couch. "Sure, what's up?"

Lara walked to the couch, and Brian joined her.

"Daddy, please try to fix things with Mom. I'm really scared."

"That's what you came here for? Look, we've been over this a thousand times," he said. "It's not that simple." Brian shifted his gaze away. She seemed so sad, and he knew nothing he would say would make her feel better.

"Dad, I know I've messed things up. Look, I see both of you every day. And she's getting better and you're getting worse. If you would just talk to her... "

"Can we change the subject?" Brian stood and walked to the window.

"You won't be able to rely on me forever."

Brian turned back to her. "What are you talking about? You're just a kid." He walked back to where she sat and bent down. "I don't rely on you, I just love being around you. Is that a crime?"

Lara kissed him on the cheek. "I gotta go."

"Yeah, that's probably a good idea. I'll see you tonight."

"Bye, Daddy. I love you."

Lara crossed the room, waved, and disappeared behind the door.

Brian walked back to his desk and pulled the bottle back out of the drawer. He didn't take the time to fill a cup; he unscrewed the lid and took a swig.

You're not going to make it.

He tried to replace the lid, but his hand shook. Brian reached in his drawer and pulled out a gun he'd purchased for protection. He held it up in the light. It appeared mighty in his hand. He rubbed the barrel against his cheek and squeezed his eyes shut. He pulled the hammer back.

The phone rang.

Brian rocketed out of his chair. The gun dropped from his hand and rattled on the desk. He stared at the phone, unsure if he should answer it. He wiped the sweat from his palms and slowly lifted the receiver to his ear.

"Hello?"

"Brian?" Ray asked.

"Oh...hi."

"Are you free for lunch today?"

Brian rolled his eyes. "No, I have plans. Maybe some other time."

"OK. Some other time."

Brian placed the receiver back on the hook and finished off his drink. He uncocked the gun, stuck the weapon in his pocket, turned off his lamp and headed for the door.

Something stopped him. He couldn't risk being caught. Brian pulled the gun out of his jacket pocket and placed it in the desk drawer. Soon he would use it, but first he would keep his promise to his daughter.

ॐ◌

After a day at the bar, Brian made his way through traffic, keeping an eye on the digital display on his dashboard. As usual, he was running late. He just hoped he didn't miss anything important. With Rhonda's condition, he knew that Lara needed him more than ever.

The light turned green, and Brian pulled into the Madison Middle School parking lot. He struggled to find a space, but finally found one on the back side of the school.

This was the first time he'd been on the campus since he was in the eighth grade. Back then, it had been a junior high school. He looked around at the mint green buildings and marveled at how much bigger they seemed then.

Brian followed the red signs pointing to the gymnasium. Inside were tables filled with cardboard displays, test tubes, mini volcanoes, and plant experiments.

Parents talked with teachers and students mingled by the far wall.

Brian searched for Lara. He didn't see her hanging out with the students, so he decided to find someone who could direct him to her homeroom teacher.

"You look lost," a woman said from behind him.

He turned around. "Um, yes. I am trying to find my daughter."

"Maybe I can help you. I'm Mrs. McGrath, the principal here at Madison Middle. What grade is your daughter in?"

"Sixth."

"And do you know what category she is in?"

Brian scratched his head. "Category?"

"For the science fair."

Brian looked around at the tables. "Oh, I thought this was a parent/teacher night."

"No, it's our annual science fair."

"Oh." Brian said. "Well, are all the students included?"

The woman smiled. "Why of course. We just break

them up into the different science categories. Biology. Chemistry. Astronomy. Geology."

Brian put up his hand. "I get it. But I'm not sure what category she would be in."

"That's fine." The principal lifted a clipboard to her chest. "Just tell me her name and I'll look it up."

"Lara Manifold."

"Hmm? Doesn't sound familiar, but let me just check..." She flipped through her list. "I'm sorry, what's her name?"

"Lara. Lara Manifold."

The woman checked again, and then shook her head. "I'm sorry, but no Lara Manifold attends here."

"That's impossible!" Brian snapped.

"I'm sorry sir, but I think you're at the wrong school."

Brian shook his head. "There must be some mistake. Maybe someone left her name off the list."

"This list comes straight from our database. I assure you, it's accurate."

"It can't be!" Brian snapped.

The woman jumped back and glanced around uncomfortably.

"Look, maybe there's a problem with your computer," Brian said in an attempt to calm himself and find a logical reason for the confusion.

The woman shook her head. "You said you thought tonight's activity was a parent/teacher conference. Apparently, you've got the wrong school."

Brian looked around, desperate. "But I've dropped my daughter off at this school a thousand times. This is where she attends."

"I don't know what to say, Mr. Manifold. She doesn't attend here. I'm truly sorry."

Brian stumbled to where a group of girls stood. "Do any of you know Lara Manifold?"

Wide-eyed, they looked at each other and shook their heads.

Heat radiated through Brian's skin. "I know my daughter attends here!" he shouted. "What's wrong with you people?"

The principal looked at the security guard posted at the gym entrance. "Sir, I'm going to have to ask you to leave," she said.

Brian followed her gaze. It had to be a mistake. His daughter went to this school. He'd dropped her off here numerous times. *What does this mean?*

The faces blurred like a Monet painting. Brian thought he might pass out. He wiped his forehead with his jacket sleeve. "I'm sorry. Maybe you're right."

He stumbled past the other parents, knocking into several on his way out.

The security guard followed close, but stopped at the curb.

Brian staggered to his car. Trepidation saturated his chest. He couldn't breathe. His body shook like mad. The ground tilted. His insides retched into his throat, sending the contents of his stomach onto the wheel of his car. *I have to get home.*

He propped against his car door and pushed the remote. It unlocked. Using the vehicle as a brace, he impelled his unwilling body inside. Vomit clung to the side of his face; his clothes were wet from sweat. He blinked. He could not see clear enough to drive.

Brian closed his eyes and tried to focus on his daughter's face.

His heart fluttered. He had to get home. Shaking, he placed the key in the ignition and started the car. He reached into the glove box, pulled out a restaurant napkin, and wiped his eyes. He could see the road. *Good enough*. He placed the car into drive.

20

Brian flung the front door open. "Lara?"

Silence.

He went to his bedroom.

Rhonda slept.

Of course. He closed the door and headed for the kitchen. "Lara?"

Nothing.

Brian steadily walked up the stairway. "Lara?" He knocked.

Still no sound.

Slowly, he pushed the door open. The room was vacant. He flipped on a table lamp by the door. The scene confused him. In the corner sat a crib and next to it, a changing table and a rocking chair. He turned around to see if he had entered the wrong door. But he knew only one door led to the loft. Surely, this wasn't his teenage daughter's bedroom.

A small light came from the adjacent bathroom to the nursery. He pushed the door open. Just like in his dream, Rhonda lay in the tub, covered in blood.

Horrified, Brian rushed to the tub, and placed her head in his arms. Her hair was matted with sweat and blood, her skirt, once soft white, was now burgundy with stain. "Rhonda, what's happened to you?"

"It's too late," she whispered. "Call 911."

This couldn't be happening. Surely, she'd be OK. His tears mixed with hers. He pulled her head to his chest and kissed her forehead.

Rhonda tried to talk, but her lips barely moved.

Brian staggered to the phone and fumbled with the numbers.

"Emergency Operator. What is your emergency?"

Panicked, Brian said, "I'm not sure. My wife is covered in blood."

The operator tried to pacify him. "Calm down, sir. I need you to tell me what happened."

"I don't know."

"Is she still breathing?"

Brian passed out.

❧

Brian awoke to a thunderous knock at the door.

Muffled sounds of a conversation drifted up the stairs.

He didn't have the strength to stand, so he inched to the door of the nursery trying to hear what was happening. Footsteps creaked on the steps. He slid back just as the door nudged open

A policeman thrust out his gun. "Freeze!"

Brian's raised his hands, covering his head. "Please, don't shoot."

"Did you call us?" the policeman asked.

It all seemed hazy, but he did remember. The officer had heard his call. Maybe he could help. Brian pointed. "She's in there."

The officer glanced towards the open door. With knees bent and pistol cocked, the uniformed man slowly crept towards the bathroom. He flipped on the switch and straightened, his expression blank. "There's nothing here."

"What?" Brian crawled to the entrance and used the door jamb to stand. "But I saw her right there."

"Saw who, sir?"

"My wife. She was covered in blood."

The police officer nodded towards Rhonda, now standing in the door of the nursery.

"Rhonda?" Brian cried.

Tears ran down Rhonda's cheek. She crossed to him. Together, they crumpled to the floor.

"You're OK?" he said.

She wiped his face. "Yes, dear, I'm OK."

"But I saw you covered in blood."

"Oh, Brian—" Rhonda sighed. "That happened almost six months ago. Not today."

"I don't remember."

She titled her head, her expression confused. "Don't you remember? That's when I lost the baby."

"No!" He wrenched away. "That's impossible! I spent time with her. Every day Lara and I talked. She's grown to be such a beautiful young woman."

"No, Brian. That isn't true. Lara died at birth. We had a funeral for her just after Thanksgiving." Rhonda peered up at the police officer.

He took his cue and stepped forward. "Is he going to be OK?"

"I think so." She tried to smile. "I'm sorry about the phone call. It won't happen again."

"You'll probably need to answer some questions. Would you mind calling this number in the morning?" He handed her a card.

Rhonda nodded.

He tipped his hat and left the room.

"Where have you been for the past several months?" Rhonda asked.

Brian closed his eyes. "Waiting for you to wake up."

"Wake up? I hardly sleep anymore."

Brian rubbed his temples. "I don't understand. Every time I come home, you're sleeping."

Rhonda shook her head. "No, Brian, every time you come home you sit in your chair and stare into space for hours. You never make eye contact with me anymore. It's only at work that you seem to come alive." She took a deep breath. "I've been talking with Ray on a regular basis and…"

Brian cut her off. "What?"

"I said I've been talking to Ray about things…"

"Ha! I knew it. You two *have* been having an affair."

She slapped him. "How dare you! He's your friend and our greatest support. He's never done anything but pray for you. I'm offended that those words could even come out of your mouth."

Brian stared at her, stunned. He didn't know what to say. "I'm sorry. Everything is just so confusing right now. I think I need to sleep."

She stood and motioned to help him.

Leaning on her arm, he pulled to stand.

Together, they walked down the steps and into their bedroom.

Rhonda helped him undress and lie down on the bed.

His breathing slowed, and within moments, he was asleep.

21

"Do you think you're going to make it?"

Brian opened his eyes. *Where am I?* It looked like his office. He peered around the room. *Yes, it is my office. But what am I doing here?*

"To meet with me, of course."

Brian turned and saw the beast covering the couch.

"Why are you still in my head? I figured out your dark secret. I'm OK, now."

The beast laughed. "Are you?"

"Look, I know that my daughter died six months ago and that she was only a figment of my imagination. Your riddle now makes sense. I get that she wasn't real."

The demon howled. "You get nothing! You're nothing but an idiot."

"How dare you call me names!" Heated, Brian trembled. "I don't want you in my life anymore. Leave my wife and me alone, and give us peace!"

The beast slithered over the side of the couch. "I'm afraid you don't have the power to get rid of me, nor do I have the power to give you peace."

Brian grabbed a lamp and ran at the beast. He swung at its repugnant head, but missed. The inertia caused him to fall back and smack his head on a small end table.

The beast roared even louder. Its mirth rumbled,

causing the windows to shake.

"You absurd human," the beast hissed. "You can't harm me."

Brian stumbled back. "What do you want from me?"

The demon leaned forward. "To die."

"But why?"

"Then you'll be ours for good."

Brian crumpled to his knees. "What is your name, demon?"

"My name is Guilt."

❧❦

Brian woke up. His whole body ached. He turned over and looked at the other side of the bed. Rhonda was not there. He struggled to stand. Every muscle screamed to stay put. He touched the back of his head and winced. The night before was foggy, but he didn't remember the wound. He started to open the bedroom door, when Rhonda entered.

"What are you doing out of bed?"

Brian smiled and kissed her.

"What was that for?" she asked, reflecting his smile.

"I've missed you," he said.

She pointed to the bed with mock authority. "I'll bring you some juice, but you need to rest. Doctor's orders."

"What doctor?"

"Me." She left the room and Brian chuckled. Rhonda was actually ABD—all but dissertation. She had planned to finish her doctorate in English before she got pregnant, but that whole experience changed a lot of things.

After a few minutes, she entered with a glass of orange juice and a plate of warm biscuits with boysenberry jam.

Brian took the tray and leaned back on the pillow. He took a bite. "I have patients to attend to. You know that I can't stay home for long."

Rhonda sat next to him, but didn't meet his gaze. "Ray is taking your case load until you are well enough to return."

Brian rolled his eyes.

"Now stop. I don't know what's with you two, but he loves you. He always has."

"He became my boss."

"So," she said.

Brian swallowed some juice. The sweet liquid seemed to clear his head. "He isn't the same, that's all."

Rhonda chuckled. "No, I think it's you who changed."

Brian set the glass down. "I haven't changed."

"Brian Dale Manifold," she said with simulated anger, "I have known you for more than thirteen years. And you aren't the same man. You're hardly the man who went to college with Ray. You're definitely not the man I married nine years ago, or for that matter, the man who spawned my child almost *two* years ago. You've changed a great deal."

Brian stared at her, and then sighed. "I promise you. I haven't changed as much as you think." He handed her the dish and climbed out of bed. "Thanks for breakfast. I think I'll take a shower."

"Brian, we really need to talk about what happened last night."

"Later." He closed the bathroom door and leaned

against it. The last thing he wanted to do was relive that nightmare.

❧❦

Danielle purchased a raspberry mocha at the cafeteria, and then sat on a brick wall outside the hospital. The sun had yet to rise and the air felt chilly. She took a sip of the hot coffee and focused on the warmth it brought. The creamy texture tasted good. She hadn't had a foo-foo drink in a while. Usually it was the sludge the doctors made in the lounge.

"Hey," Ray said.

Danielle glanced up. "You're here early."

"Can we talk?"

She nodded toward the space next to her on the wall.

"I think it's going to be a pretty day, huh?"

Danielle glanced out over the parking lot. An orange hue began to peek over the horizon. "Yeah, most likely. Though I wish it would rain."

"Yeah, it's been a while." He scraped his toe against the cement. "I owe you an apology. You were right."

She pivoted sideways to see him better. "Maybe, but I didn't have the right to yell at you. Sorry."

Their gazes locked.

"No, I need someone like you in my life. I'm not thinking rationally these days."

"How is he?"

Ray's countenance fell. "Not well, I'm afraid."

"I'm sorry." It seemed to be the only thing she knew how to say in regards to Brian. "I'll be praying for him."

"Thanks." Ray's eyes grew huge. He stood.

Danielle followed his line of sight.

A few doors down Brian entered the building.

"He's not supposed to be here." Ray glanced back to Danielle. "We'll have to finish this later. I have to go."

"Of course."

He hurried to the entrance and disappeared behind the sliding glass door.

The sudden urge to pray returned. *Lord, whatever this is, please be in it.*

❧

"Brian, what are you doing here?" Ray followed Brian into his office. "You should go home. You aren't ready to see any clients right now."

"Let me decide that, OK?" Brian laid his briefcase on the desk.

Ray shook his head. "I'm afraid I can't let you do that."

"Why?"

Ray swallowed. "Because it's now out of my hands."

Brian stepped closer to Ray and stared him in the eye. "What does that mean?"

"It means…" Ray took a deep breath. He didn't want to be this person, but he had no choice. It was his job. "It means that the board has decided to place you on suspension. You're not allowed to see patients until a full investigation has been conducted."

"What?" Brian snapped, causing Ray to jump. "They can't do that."

"I'm afraid they already have. Their plan was to

send you to counseling, but after last night, they decided to also revoke your license."

Brian crossed his arms and leaned on his left hip. "How would they know about last night?"

Ray didn't answer.

Heat augmented Brian's neck. "Rhonda called you, didn't she?" Brian moved inches from Ray's face. "And you just *had* to tell them."

"Look, I didn't want to, but yes, you're right." Ray backed up. "I had to. It's my job. Not that last night really changed anything. It was going to happen, anyway."

Brian shook a finger at Ray. "I always knew you were out to destroy me."

"That's simply not true. I'm *for* you, not against you."

"Then prove it. Help me out here. Let me prove that I'm not crazy. I've had a hard time dealing with the death of my infant child. Who wouldn't?"

Ray frowned. "I know it has been hard. I've said that from day one, but I kept telling you to get help, and you refused. I'm willing to work with you, but you need to take some time off. I'll see what I can do. But for now, you need to go home."

Brian paced. "So, I have no choice?"

"Not right now. I'm sorry."

Brian turned to Ray, his shoulders hunched, resigned to the news. "Can I just hang out here for a while? I need to get some things in order before I take time off. Especially if I am going to be gone for any length of time."

Ray nodded. "Fine, but do yourself and Rhonda a favor."

"What's that?"

"Talk to your wife, Brian. Work through this together. It's too much for one man to handle alone."

"We're working on it."

"And then... "

"Yes, Ray?"

"Talk to God."

Brian didn't respond.

Ray patted him on the back and left Brian to his office.

જ્જ

Brian lay back on the couch and stared at the ceiling. He recognized the dark, sinister terrain that inhabited his dreams. He didn't care about the locality this time; he simply wanted to confront the evil lord that sought to destroy him. "I want you out of my life." He yelled to coagulated darkness. "I want you to leave Rhonda and me alone."

Smoke rose from the floor and in the distance, a crimson light reflected off the hideous creature's hunched back. The beast snarled and a sharp aroma of sulfur permeated the air.

"So you want to be left alone?" The beast cackled. "You still don't get it, do you? I don't care what you want. It's what my master wants. And he wants you."

"Why me?" Brian grabbed his chest. "Why not somebody else?"

"Because," the beast hissed, "you gave us the key."

"What key?"

જ્જ

"Doc?"

Brian felt something knocking his side. Opening his eyes, Jake came into focus. "Jake?" Brian stretched. "What are you doing here?"

"Don't we have an appointment?"

Brian sat up. "Well, to be honest, Jake. I'm not allowed to see you anymore."

"What?" Jake clenched his jaw and fists. "Why?"

"Apparently, I'm on suspension."

Jake shook his head and sat on the couch, arms crossed, determination on his face. "I don't care. I need your help."

"I can't help you, Jake." Brian rubbed his temples. A migraine lay imminent to the near future.

"Yes, you can. And will. I'm not going anywhere until you do." Jake jumped up, grabbed the Bible and leapt back on the couch.

"Look, kid. I really care about you. We've had some interesting sessions, and I believe that you're progressing. But I just don't have the right to help you any longer. Someone else may be better for you and—"

"I don't want anyone else. Please, just help me this one last time. Just talk to me." Jake tossed the Bible on the couch and folded his hands in a plea. "Come on, Doc. Just one more hour. That's all I ask."

Brian looked at the door, and then at his watch. His heart raced. He stared at the desperate, pale adolescent. He'd never had to turn away a patient. It made him angry and sad at the same time. "I just can't."

Jake's voice rose, agitated. "But you have to. You promised to be there for me until I got better. Well, I ain't better, Doc. So, you've got to help me!"

"I have to let you go, Jake." Brian grabbed a few framed pictures of Rhonda off the shelf and placed them inside his briefcase. "I have to get well myself. Don't you understand?"

"No, I won't let you just throw me out. We had a deal, remember?"

"And things change."

Jake paced, fists clenched at his side, jaw flexing. "You can't do this. I promise, you'll regret it if you do."

"Settle down."

"Settle down? You're tossing me out as if I was an obsolete computer." Jake pointed his finger at Brian. "I won't let you! You're going to listen to me."

"Jake, please. I can't help you. Don't you understand? I have to let everyone go. Not just you—but all my patients. I have to get well."

Just inches from Brian's face, Jake stopped and eyeballed Brian.

Brian's heart pounded.

"Have you admitted it yet?" Jake asked.

Brian stepped back. "Admitted what?"

"That you killed her?"

"Killed who? I think we're talking about you, Jake."

"No! No! No!" Jake stomped his foot like a toddler. "Don't you do that! Don't you dare deny it again! You want to get better, right? Then admit you killed her!"

Terror griped Brian's throat. "Jake, you're scaring me. Now, just calm down. I haven't killed anybody."

Jake walked to the couch and hurled Brian's Bible across the room. "Yes, you have!"

"Fine!" Brian held up his hands in surrender. "Who have I killed? Who?"

Jake smiled a sinister smile that sent a chill down Brian's neck. "Your daughter, stupid. You killed your own daughter."

Brian collapsed to the floor. "I didn't kill my daughter," he whispered.

"Oh, yeah? If it weren't for you, wouldn't your baby have been born alive and well?"

Brian shuddered. Perspiration teemed down his face, his heart pumped madly.

"Admit it, Doc. You killed your own baby girl."

The world swam, and Brian was thrust back six months...

"Honey, where are you?" Brian yelled from downstairs.

"I'm here." Rhonda yelled from the landing above. "I thought you weren't going to be home for a while."

He smiled. "I lied."

"So, I see."

Brian bounded up the stairs, took his wife in his arms and drew her into a deep kiss.

She pushed away. "You've been drinking."

"I know. Don't be mad. It's for a good reason."

She folded her arms, apparently not convinced. "And you drove home?"

He shook his head. "No, I took a cab. But all that doesn't matter." He took her arms. He was too excited to let her anger dampen the reason for his real high. "What's the one thing that would make me the happiest man on earth?"

"Having a baby?"

He laughed. "Besides that?"

"I don't know."

"Come on, think," he said.

"I guess, getting published?"

"Yes."

"What?" Rhonda shrieked.

"Yes! I'm going to be published." He flung his arms out and bowed.

"But how?" she asked.

"The publishing company that edited my dissertation decided that my research would make a great book." He beamed. "Can you believe it? I'm going to be published!"

"Oh my! That's...that's just so awesome!"

He grabbed Rhonda in his arms and spun her around, but her weight caught him off balance and everything slowed. He reached for her, but missed.

Rhonda hurled down the steps. Her head smacked the railing and her body went limp. One. Two. Three. Four. Her body tumbled off each step. Five. Six. Seven. Turning, twisting.

It was as if time stopped, and Brian could do nothing to move in it.

At the bottom step, she lay mangled. Blood seeped down her face and hair.

Brian ran down the stairs, stumbling over most of them. Everything in him wanted to scoop her up, but he knew better. "Rhonda!" he screamed. "Don't you die on me!" He patted his jacket for his cell phone. As usual, he must have left it in his car. He stood to leave.

Rhonda moaned, "Wait."

"You're alive!"

"Something is wrong." She clenched her stomach with a balled fist. "Take me to the bathroom."

"But I shouldn't move you."

"The baby's coming!"

Brian fumbled to pick her up, and managed to transfer her to their master bathroom. He laid her gently in the tub and grabbed a pillow for her head.

"Call 911."

Brian nodded dumbly.

Rhonda appeared to be struggling to stay conscious. Her white dress hung heavy and wet in a pool of blood. She screamed.

Brian yelled frantically in the phone, "My wife... she's nine months pregnant and fell down a flight of stairs. She's in the tub about to give birth." He paced, nausea and adrenaline coursed through his body. "Shouldn't I just give you my address so you can get here and figure all that out yourself?"

Rhonda screamed again.

Brian entered the doorway and his face turned white.

A baby lay at his wife's feet, blue and still.

"I can't reach her!" Rhonda cried, pointing at the end of the tub.

With trembling hands, Brian lifted the small child to Rhonda's chest.

"I don't think she's breathing," she wheezed, stroking the blood-matted hair of her baby daughter.

Brian buckled to the tile, sobs shaking his whole body.

Rhonda stared at the blue, lifeless child in her arms.

A knock came at the door.

"That's probably the ambulance," Brian said weakly. He lifted to his feet in a zombie-like daze.

A moment later, several paramedics enveloped their bathroom. They put Rhonda and their daughter, Lara, onto a gurney and whisked them off to an emergency room in the city.

They declared Lara dead at 9:05 PM on June fifth. It was one of the worst days of their lives.

Brian stayed with Rhonda, while they treated her

for a slight concussion and some internal bleeding. After five days in the hospital, they allowed her to go home.

But life at the Manifold home changed.

Brian remembered very little after. Often he would stare at the wall for hours at a time. Eventually, he stopped talking to Rhonda altogether.

22

"How did you know?" Brian asked.

Jake laughed. "You still don't know who I am, do you?"

"You're Jake. Juvenile Delinquent. Accused murderer. And I'm your therapist." Brian rubbed his eyes. "Look, I think you should go. It really isn't a good idea for you to be here."

Jake jumped up. "No, don't start that again. I'm not leaving."

"Please, Jake, I need to relax."

"I suppose you need a drink, right?"

Brian raised an eyebrow. "What?"

"Or maybe it isn't alcohol that you seek, but the sensual arms of my girlfriend, Krissy?"

Brian fumed. "You little twit. Have you been following me?"

"Are you going to get rid of me the way you got rid of your daughter?"

Brian pointed to the door. "That's enough! Get out of my office."

"No!" Jake walked toward Brian, chest out, hands in his pockets. "I'm not leaving."

"Then I'm calling security." Brian crossed to the phone.

Jake lifted his hands in mock surrender. "Whoa. Fine I'll go," he said, and then looked at Brian with a glimmer of mischievousness. "For now."

As soon as Jake was out the door, Brian snatched up the phone. "Hello? Bernie. This is Dr. Brian Manifold. There is a patient who just left my office. I need you to make sure that he leaves the premises. He's about six-two, with dark spiky hair. He's wearing a black trench coat and combat boots. He has about four piercings on his face and a tattoo of a spider web on the back of his neck."

"Sure thing, Dr. Manifold," Bernie said.

"Thank you." Brian hung up.

His heart pounded. He walked to the door and locked it. He grabbed a box and started filling it with books from his shelf. He was almost done packing when the phone rang.

"Hello?"

"Your man never checked out." Bernie said.

Brian felt sick. "What do you mean, he never checked out?"

"We never saw him come by, sir."

Fear clutched his throat. "I'll need an escort in about five minutes."

"Yes, sir."

"Thank you." Brian hung up. His door was locked and they would help him to his car. Nothing to worry about. Brian grabbed the last picture from his desk and surveyed the room. The sight of the bare walls washed him in despair.

He rubbed his hands together and set the last box in the corner. A courier would pick them up tomorrow morning. Brian snapped his briefcase closed, turned off his lamp, and walked to the door.

Someone knocked.

"Who is it?" Brian's voice trembled.

"Security."

Brian breathed a sigh of relief and unlocked the door.

Jake stood in the doorway, red faced, eyes piercing, exerting quick breaths.

Adrenaline surged through Brian's body. "Jake? What are you still doing here?"

The young man's chin rested at his chest, but his eyes focused up at Brian. He said nothing, but pressed forward.

"You need to leave, son."

Jake laughed an eerie laugh. "You don't get it, do you?"

"Get what, Jake?" Brian stumbled as he backed up.

"I'm not that easy to get rid of."

"Look, I want to help you. Really I do." Brian used the furniture to help him retreat. "But I can't. It wasn't by choice that I lost my license."

Jake inched closer to Brian. "That's where you're wrong, Doc. It's *all* your fault. If you weren't so messed up, then you'd still be able to help me."

Brian nodded briskly. "Yes, you're exactly right. I'm a horrible mess. You'd do better in someone else's care. Someone without all my baggage."

Jake pushed Brian into a corner and slammed his hand on the wall next to Brian's shoulder. "No one can help me," Jake said.

Brian stared at the pitiable adolescent before him and wasn't sure if he felt fear, or sympathy. Probably both. Brian inched past Jake and made a beeline for the phone. "I'm afraid I'll have to call security."

Jake followed close behind him. Brian picked up the receiver, but Jake shot the phone with a pistol.

Brian jumped back, ghostly white. "Where'd you get the gun, Jake?"

"I'm here to get help, and you're going to help me." Jake motioned for Brian to move to the chair. "Now sit down!"

Brian reached inside his desk drawer, but the gun was gone.

"You don't think I could just bring a gun in here, do you?" Jake smirked. "Now do as I said. Sit over there!"

Brian tripped over own his feet and his chin hit the arm of the couch. He wailed in pain.

Jake ignored him and paced. "Why'd you even become a doctor?"

Brian blinked. Jake's words would not register. "I'm sorry, what did you say?"

Jake obviously lacked patience. He waved the gun around and repeated his question. "I asked you, why'd you become a doctor?"

"To help people."

"That's the easy answer. Give me the real one."

Brian looked away and sighed. "My mom was manic-depressive. I never thought anyone did enough to help her. I thought maybe I could change things."

"But you messed up. You didn't help anyone. You're crazier than all your patients combined."

Brian shook his head. "No, I've helped a lot of people...and I'm not crazy. I'm just going through a rough time."

Jake howled. "Ha! First you invent a teenage daughter and now you have no idea who I am. Tell me, Doc, do you dream about demons, too?"

Brian's head swelled. He tried to focus, but the room spun like he was on a Ferris wheel. "How do you know all that?"

Jake belted out a wretched laugh. "Poor little Dr.

Manifold. Went off and killed his own baby and now he can't function."

"I'm warning you, Jake, stop talking about that!"

"You wanted me to talk, so I'll talk. *We* killed her, Brian. *We* did."

"What?"

"Your daughter. You and I killed her."

"That's impossible."

Jake laughed. "You know how you can help me, Doc? You can make the pain go away. You can just stop living." Jake put the barrel to his own temple.

Brian's eyes went wide. "Jake, please put the gun down!"

"I'm so sick of feeling guilty. I just want to live happily ever after—to wake up in the morning and feel my wife in my arms—to know that we have a child growing up in the other room."

"Put the gun down, and then maybe I can start to help you sort things out."

Jake yelled, "No! We've been doing that for months. I'm tired of talking. We don't talk. You won't let us. You make me read that Bible, thinking that will take away the pain and guilt of what we did. But it won't." Jake leveled the gun at Brian. "Say goodbye."

&⁓

Dr. Raven's eyes went wide. "Dr. Manifold, put the gun down."

Brian held the gun to his own temple and trembled. Sweat and tears poured down his face. His body convulsed. "I can't do this anymore. Don't you understand? I have to get rid of all of them. If I don't, I can never get well."

"If you shoot, Doctor, you will cease to exist."

Brian's knees buckled.

Dr. Raven walked his way, but halted when Brian aimed the gun at him. "Brian, please." Dr. Raven pleaded. "We can talk about this. This isn't going to end well. You will lose everything you care about."

"Oh, so now you'll call me Brian. Now that you're looking down the barrel of a gun you want to be friends."

"Look, I'm here for you. We can work this out."

Brian shook his head violently. "No! You're about to tell the board to take away my license, right?"

Dr. Raven paused.

Brian cocked the gun.

The doctor nodded. "Yes, I'm afraid I'll have to."

"I need my job. It keeps me sane."

"I assure you, Dr. Manifold, that's not the case."

Brian recoiled.

"It sounds like things are getting better at home."

"No, things aren't better because you're still in here." Brian tapped the gun on his temple, and then directed it again at Dr. Raven.

"Please, Doctor, let me help you. If you give me the gun, then maybe we can sort through this mess and…"

Dr. Raven took a step toward the phone.

Brian pulled the trigger. Dr. Raven reached for his stomach and went out of focus. Brian's stomach burned. He looked down and screamed. He was bleeding.

Everything went black.

23

Danielle flipped on a desk lamp and walked behind the desk. The office felt still, just as she liked it. But the peace wouldn't last. The rest of the staff would be along soon to start another—

An explosive blast shattered the quiet.

Her heart lurched as she dropped to the floor. *What was that?* She listened hard in the soft light, afraid to stand. Silence rang in her ears. Slowly, she stood and inched out from behind her desk.

A single light glowed from under Dr. Manifold's door. Did she dare go down there? She eyed the elevator and then her purse. Leaving the building seemed better. But what if he was hurt? Compassion— or maybe curiosity—won out. On tiptoes, she crept forward, her rubber soles squeaking on the tile floor.

"Hello? Dr. Manifold? Are you in there?" Her heart hammered. She lifted a hand to the door, and then closed it in a fist, hesitant to discover what lay within.

The receptionist's telephone echoed down the dark hallway, almost sending her into cardiac arrest. Swallowing, she pushed the door. "Dr. Manifold? Brian?"

A groan sounded from behind the couch.

She leaned forward, keeping her feet planted.

A lock of the doctor's brown hair was draped across the arm of the couch.

"Dr. Manifold, are you OK?" She stepped around the couch and stared in horror.

A diminutive crimson river flowed from the doctor's ear, and a gun hung loosely from his hand.

Timidly, she grabbed the weapon and tossed it into a nearby chair, then pulled off her sweater and pressed it against his wound, before checking his pulse with her free hand. *Weak.*

She pulled her cell phone out. Unable to remember the direct line to the ER on the bottom floor, she dialed the shack below. "Security?" Danielle yelled once someone answered. "Hurry and get up here! Dr. Manifold shot himself!"

In what seemed like hours, two security guards armed with only nightsticks and brawn bolted through the office door.

"What happened?" Bernie, the older of the two guards, ran over and knelt next to them.

"I heard a gunshot." Her lip quivered. She blinked back tears and pointed to the nearby chair. "The gun is there."

The guard lifted his radio. "Mac, get someone in ER to bring up a gurney. We have an injured man and shots fired."

The radio squawked. "Say again."

"Bring a gurney from ER. One of the doctors has been shot!"

"Yes, sir."

The other guard, Les, peeked over the couch with one eyebrow raised. Instantly, his face became grass green. He bolted for a trashcan by the door and expelled the contents of his stomach.

Dani grimaced.

"Les, why don't you check the other offices?"

Bernie asked.

The man nodded without saying a word and stepped into the hallway.

Danielle wanted to join him. Nausea fluttered through her stomach, as well.

"Did you see what happened?" Bernie searched her face.

She shook her head, her gaze lingering on the doorway. "I just heard the shot, and found him with the gun."

"I see." He nodded and put a couple fingers to the inert man's neck. "His pulse is weak."

An elevator bell chimed in the hallway and clear relief crossed the guard's face.

Hers, too, she was sure. It took everything in her not to bolt. It wasn't as if she'd never seen blood before. But this was Brian—her colleague, and once, a friend.

Les entered. "All clear."

Two medical personnel entered with a gurney.

Danielle stood and stared at her scarlet hands. "May I go home?"

"I'm sorry. Not yet." Bernie offered a tight smile. "The cops will want to talk to you. Why don't you go with Les to the ER waiting room, and I'll let the police know that you're there." He faced his partner. "Let her clean up and get some coffee. And wipe your face." Bernie motioned his hand over his own face in rapid circles. "You've got stuff, um... "

"Yes, sir." Les wiped at his face with the back of his brown sleeve. "I'm sorry, sir. I've just never seen anything like this."

"No worries, son. It's your first week." Bernie patted Les's back. "Just take care of the lady, OK? I'll work this out."

Les nodded and faced her. "Come on, miss."

Call Ray. She pulled at her purse and fumbled with the zipper. Her hands were shaking so bad, the leather bag toppled to the floor. Lipsticks and coins rolled around the moving cart.

Les bent down and helped her gather her stuff.

"Sorry, I was looking for my phone."

The guard lifted the black rectangle in the air.

"Thank you," she said, with a half-hearted smile.

"Sure."

The elevator slid open.

In the waiting room, people waited. A man sat with a bag of ice to his head. A mother rocked a crying baby. An elderly couple coughed in the corner.

Danielle passed them all, and walked outside. The cool air instantly soothed her. It took three tries, but she finally managed to dial the right number.

"Hello?" Ray's voice was raised in inquiry.

"Ray, it's Danielle." She sniffed. "Are you still in the building?"

"Yeah, I'm in the lounge. Are you OK?"

She took a deep breath. "Something awful has happened."

❧

"Ah, so you have decided to join me?"

Brian opened his eyes. He lay against a cement floor in what appeared to be a damp basement. The beast hovered over him. Brian suffered from the beast's hot, foul breath on his face. "You?" Brian sneered. "I thought I was rid of you."

The demon hissed. "On the contrary, it appears

you may be with us for a very long time."

Brian tried to sit up, but his abdomen throbbed. He looked down and saw blood.

The beast laughed.

"I'm bleeding."

"Yes." The creature sneered. "You shot yourself."

"You mean Jake shot *me*."

"You still don't get it, do you?"

Brian looked away.

"You brainless being. You're Jake. Jake is you."

"What?" Brian glared at the hideous beast. "That's ridiculous."

"Is it?"

"Of course, it's absurd. You are insinuating that I have Dissociative Identity Disorder, or that maybe I'm schizophrenic."

"Or that you're possessed."

"I'm nothing."

"When you pulled the trigger, whom did you aim at?"

Brian closed his eyes and tried to recall the scene. His eyes shot open. "I shot Dr. Raven."

"Yes," hissed the beast. "But... "

"But then, why am *I* shot?"

"Precisely the question isn't it, *Doc*?"

❧❦

Ray took a deep breath before pushing send on his cell phone.

"Hello?" Rhonda answered on the first ring.

"Rhonda? It's Ray."

"Oh, thank goodness, Ray. I've been worried sick about Brian. He was supposed to be a few—"

"Rhonda, I need you to listen to me."

"OK."

He squeezed his eyes shut. "Brian's been shot."

For moment, the line seemed dead. "I'm sorry, what did you say?"

"He's in surgery right now, and they need you to fill out some paperwork."

"No!" Her muffled cries were followed by a thump.

"Rhonda? Rhonda!"

"I'll be there!" The phone connection died.

Ray stared at the screen for a second. Never had he felt so hopeless. "Lord, please help my friend." He grabbed his jacket, stuffed his phone in his back pocket, and ran out of the office. He didn't wait for the elevator. He bounded down the stairs taking three or more at a time. At the bottom step, his face flooded with tears. He took in a deep breath, wiped his face on his sleeve and slammed down the door handle. He crossed to the front desk, and waited for the nurse to look up.

"Can I help you?" she asked.

"Yes." He flashed his hospital badge. "One of our employees was brought in here a few hours ago. I need to talk with his doctor."

"Are you a doctor here?"

"Yes. I work on the seventh floor."

That did it. The nurse smiled. "You're management, then?"

Ray nodded.

"What's the employee's name?"

"Dr. Brian Manifold."

The nurse clicked a few keys on her computer and nodded. "Yes, he was brought in with a gunshot wound to his abdomen."

"Do they know who shot him?"

"Apparently, it was self-inflicted."

Ray felt the color drain from his face.

"A blonde woman and a security guard checked him in."

Danielle. "Did they leave?"

"The security guard left right away, and the woman is over there." She pointed to Danielle leaning against a drinking fountain, makeup smeared, nose red. She met his gaze.

He held up a finger indicating he'd be right there. "May I speak to his doctor?"

"I'll check." The nurse exited a glass door behind her and disappeared.

He crossed to Danielle. "Hi," he said softly.

She fell into his arms and sobbed. "When I saw him…" She trailed off.

"I understand. It's too much for anyone to see."

She pulled back and looked at him. "Will he be OK?"

Ray lightly wiped a tear from her cheek. "I hope so."

The desk nurse returned.

"Give me a second," he told Danielle, withdrawing from her arms.

"Certainly," she said.

"I'm sorry, Dr. Jensen," the nurse said, "but he's unable see you right now. He's in surgery with your friend. But if you'd like to wait, he's agreed to see you when he's done."

"Thank you."

Ray turned back to Danielle, and escorted her to the waiting room, his legs numb. *What had the nurse said? Self-inflicted? Shot in the stomach?* The words rang in his head like a clanging cymbal.

24

Ray sat in the far back corner with Danielle. The white tiled room was strewn with wounded people.

Rhonda shot through the entrance double glass doors, gaze frantic. "I received a call that my husband was brought here."

Ray stood and crossed to her.

"Your husband's name?"

"Dr. Brian Manifold."

The woman looked at her screen, punched a few keys, and said, "Yes, he's in surgery right now. You can wait in the lobby."

"Wait! I don't know what's happened! I need someone to tell me something. "

"I'm sorry, ma'am. Unfortunately, I'm not authorized to give you any more information, but I'll let the doctors know you're here."

"Rhonda."

Tears and mascara lined her face. She reached out and fell into his arms.

He patted her back, not really sure how to console her. After she relaxed some, he pulled back. "You know, I'm here for you."

"They haven't told me a thing. Do you know what happened?"

He guided her to a nearby chair.

"I need to know more. I need to know if he's going to live. Can you please find *something* out?"

He knelt at her feet, and took her hand.

"Is he dead?" Her eyes seemed to search his.

"Rhonda…" Ray cleared his throat. "He shot himself in the stomach."

Rhonda pulled back. "Shot *himself*?"

"Yes. Danielle found him."

Rhonda glanced at the gorgeous blonde, and then back to Ray. "But everything was going to be OK."

He cupped his hand around hers. This conversation broke his heart. He wanted to believe it. That his friend would be just fine. He spoke more for himself than her. "He's in critical condition, but I believe he'll be OK."

Rhonda shook her head; new tears grazed her cheek. "I just don't understand. Please tell me how my husband could shoot himself."

"Have you ever heard of schizophrenia?" Ray asked.

"From movies, I guess." She shrugged. "I don't exactly have a psychology degree."

"Brian really took the loss of your child pretty bad. Worse than I think most of us assumed. We knew for a while that he was dealing with depression, and possibly hallucinations, but what he concocted was far beyond what the medical profession has seen in years." Ray sighed. "Since the accident, Brian has actually been living in a world filled with people who don't exist."

"You're not making sense. I don't understand what you're saying. How's that possible?"

"Some people have a genetic condition that predisposes them to the onset of schizophrenia or possibly DID. We believe that Brian may have one or the other."

"Did? What's that?"

"No, D-I-D. Dissociative Identity Disorder—once known as Multiple Personality Disorder."

Rhonda shook her head. "Before the accident, he was fine."

Danielle laid her hand on his shoulder.

Ray nodded, silently thanking her for the comfort, and stared back at his broken friend. "Usually psychosis of this nature is set off by life stressors or fear caused by a traumatic experience. I believe that your miscarriage and the fear about his behavior were the key. The guilt of the accident was his passport to slip out of this world and into his own reality."

"What reality?"

"There may be more personalities that we don't know about, but from what we can tell, he developed a relationship with your daughter, a patient named Jake, and a psychologist. It was this psychologist personality, Dr. Raven, who allowed him to get back to *our* reality."

"You're telling me," she said, in a sarcastic tone, "that my husband had a relationship with my dead child and it was an imaginary friend that brought him back to reality?"

"I know this is hard to understand."

"This is beyond bizarre." Rhonda covered her face with her hands.

"Maybe we should give her some time," Danielle whispered.

Ray nodded and stood.

"Why did Brian try to kill himself?" Rhonda asked.

"I guess in some desperate attempt to be alone."

"What?" Rhonda leapt to her feet. "But he shot *himself!*"

"You can't think about this the same way you think about a childhood make-believe friend. When you're a kid, the friend is invisible and over there." Ray motioned a few feet in front of him. "But when you're a paranoid schizophrenic or have DID," Ray pointed to his temple, "the person is in here."

"So he believed he was all of those people?" Rhonda asked.

"Well, yes and no. That's what's so weird about this case. With schizophrenia, one hallucinates. Hears voices, imagines things, but with Dissociative Identity Disorder, one actually believes he *is* those people. According to the text books, a person can't really have both problems, and yet Brian seems to be displaying signs of both."

"But he just stared into space. I never saw him talk to himself."

"He may have appeared catatonic to you, but for him, he was living out life through those relationships." Ray touched her hand. How could he help her? Years as a professional taught him he couldn't. The most he could do was be here. Listen and love. "I'm sorry, Rhonda."

Rhonda sat back down and wiped her eyes. "Is he awake? Is that how you know all this?"

Ray looked down at his hands.

"Ray?"

He bit his lip, not meeting her eyes.

"Ray, answer me."

"No." He swallowed, unable to look at her. This would not make her happy. "I have been putting the pieces together for a while. It was my job to evaluate him, to determine if he was still fit to counsel. He started having panic attacks, outbursts in his office, often when he was alone. He drank more than usual and was unusually paranoid that people were out to get him."

"Well, weren't they?"

Ray met her gaze. "People were worried, and obviously for a good reason. No one wanted him to get hurt. They wanted him to seek help." Ray glanced at Danielle, who offered a supportive smile. He sighed. "I told him this morning that the board revoked his license."

"What?" Rhonda yelled. "You knew all along and you didn't help him? You didn't even tell me. I'm his wife! I deserved to know. How dare you call yourself my friend?"

"Rhonda, please. I was not at liberty to talk about his case."

"Bull!" she spat.

"You know how it is. We're under strict rules of confidentiality. In a sense, Brian was my patient. I could have been fired."

"What's your job to my husband's life?"

"That's not fair."

Rhonda held Ray's gaze. "I lost my baby, my marriage is sour, and now my husband might die. Tell me, Ray, what in this whole situation has been remotely fair?"

Ray looked away, but not in time to hide his tears. "I'm sorry, Rhonda. I failed you."

∂∾ఈ

"Are you OK?" Danielle handed Ray a cup of coffee.

"Thank you." He took the cup and inhaled the

steam. "I will be."

She had never been in this kind of tragedy before. Knowing what to do or how to comfort him was a mystery. She was afraid she might say the wrong thing. She cared about this man, more than he knew, and she didn't want to hurt him. She had no idea what to do.

Talk to him. Listen to his words.

A familiar peace, God's love, settled in her heart.

"I can still remember when Brian and I became true friends. We were at this all-night study session. Everyone had downed at least two pots of coffee when Brian decided we should go buy triple espressos at the campus coffee shop. I was the only one willing to take the break and go." Ray's eyes glistened as he talked. "We went, but they were just closing up."

Danielle turned to face him.

"This cute Hispanic girl happened to walk back through the shop to get something. Brian started pounding on the window." Ray's voice wavered. He ran a hand over his face and sniffed. "He actually had enough charm not only to get the girl to open up and turn the bar back on, but he talked her into staying up with us the rest of the night. The three of us were the best of friends after that."

Her heart went out to this torn man. "Where is the girl now?" Danielle asked.

Ray offered a slight grin. "Amy is kind of my sister-in-law."

Sister-in-law? Danielle's heart stopped. "I thought you weren't married and an only child."

"Yes, and I have a mother with an enormous heart. We used to have troubled teens stay in our home all the time while I was growing up. One of my foster siblings ended up marrying Amy. He went in the Navy and they live in Bremerton, Washington, now."

"Interesting."

Ray stared at Danielle, his expression not clear.

"What?" She wiped her face. "I must be a mess."

"Actually, you're a breath of fresh air."

Heat rose in her face. "Thanks."

"No, thank you. I couldn't imagine walking through this without you by my side. You're amazing." He reached for her hand and interlaced her fingers with his.

Goosebumps ran up her arm. She felt like a young girl again. "I'm not sure I'm much good. I honestly don't know what to say."

His hand squeezed hers gently. "You're here. That's more than enough."

৵৹৵

After four cups of coffee, two packages of stale vending machine pastries, and seven trips to the bathroom, Ray was overjoyed to see Brian's surgeon emerge.

Rhonda stood first.

"Hello, I'm Dr. Porter." He shook Rhonda's hand, and then shook Ray's hand, too. He motioned for them to sit.

"Is he OK?" Rhonda asked. "Is he going to make it?"

The doctor nodded. "Your husband lost a lot of blood. We were able to pull the bullet from his stomach, but he'll have a difficult recovery. He won't be able to eat solid food for a long while, and we had to insert a bag so he could dispense waste. His recovery will depend on him and his will to survive. Considering this has been deemed a suicide attempt, I won't say that we're not concerned." The doctor pursed his lips and sighed. "Do you have any questions?"

"Can I see him?" she rasped.

"Not yet. He'll be relocated to a room upstairs later this evening. You may see him then. I advise you to get some rest." He offered her a small grin, nodded, and returned to the doors marked "Employees only."

Ray put his hand on her shoulder. "He's right, you know. You should get some rest."

Rhonda shook her head and slumped in her chair. "I don't think I can sleep until I see him."

"Yeah, I figured you'd say that. I asked Danielle to grab you some stuff. She should be here in an hour. I'll stay with you until then."

"Danielle? The woman who has been here all day." Rhonda tilted her head to the side, eyes narrowed, something she often did when she was ready to drill someone. "Are you two seeing each other?"

How did he answer that? They'd been trying for weeks, but it never seemed quite right. Even now that she was here with him, it felt strained. Awkward, even. He liked her, but it was too much to consider at the moment. "She's a good friend."

"Well, she better be nice to you, or she's history." Rhonda laid her head on his shoulder and let out a long sigh.

Ray raked a hand through her hair and nodded. "Get some sleep, Rhonda."

25

Brian tried to open his eyes. It was so dark. He feared the beast would soon claim him. His eyelids rested like sandbags. Beyond him, he heard a soothing voice. He longed to see its owner, but he simply could not open his eyes.

The speech became clearer and stronger. "And I love you. So you see, you have to get better."

Rhonda. He recognized his wife's tone. That's all the determination he needed. He labored to push his eyelids open.

"Brian?" he heard Rhonda say. "Nurse. Nurse! You have to get in here. I think he's waking up."

He saw the outline of what appeared to be a nurse's uniform.

"Yes," the nurse said, "I think he just might be trying to make it back. Let me fetch the doctor."

The image disappeared and was replaced with Rhonda's familiar shape. He couldn't tell if she was smiling or crying. He longed to yell how much he loved her, to wrap his arms around her neck. But his entire body lolled like lead. He squinted.

"How do you feel?"

Brian didn't answer. *Couldn't* answer. He tried to communicate with his eyes, but he knew he probably just looked cross-eyed.

"A doctor is on his way to look at you," Rhonda said, kissing his forehead. "You gave us quite a scare.

But I love you, darling, and I so desperately want you to get better."

A small tear trickled from the corner of Brian's eye.

She wiped it with the back of her hand just as the doctor entered.

"I see our patient has come back to us. Wonderful." The chipper medical professional grabbed the chart from the end of Brian's bed and wrote a few notes. He replaced the chart, crossed to the head of the bed, and withdrew a thin flashlight from his pocket. "Can you talk to me, Brian?" he asked, shining a light into Brian's pupils.

He wished he could, but his tongue adhered to the floor of his mouth.

The doctor nodded, picked up Brian's arm, and tapped on his hand. "Did you feel that?"

Brian felt it, but he couldn't tell him.

"Blink once for yes and twice for no."

Brian blinked once.

"What's wrong with him?" Rhonda asked concerned.

The doctor looked at her and grinned. "Don't worry, Mrs. Manifold. This is common. He just woke up from quite an experience. The drugs we gave him also aid in this. He can feel and understand me, so that's a good sign." He glanced back at Brian. "I'll be back to check on you in an hour or so." He nodded to Rhonda and left.

His wife looked tired. Brian wondered how long she'd stayed by his side. Endlessly, he was sure.

Ray entered.

Why wouldn't Ray just let them be? What more damage did he plan to do?

"Hi, Brian. I know you probably don't want to see me right now, but I really am your friend in all this."

Brian rolled his eyes. It was his only defense.

Rhonda ran her fingers through Brian's hair. "Please, Brian. He isn't the enemy. I promise."

Brian wanted to plead with her to see the truth, but he could only lie there.

"Brian, there are a few things we need to discuss, but I'll wait until you're feeling better." He looked at Rhonda. "If it's OK, I need to talk to you for a moment."

She turned to Brian. "I'll be right back," she said.

He blinked twice, but Rhonda didn't seem to notice, and left the room with the enemy.

Brian stared at the ceiling. Tears grazed his cheeks. He felt so unsure of what had happened. The last thing he clearly remembered was finding Rhonda covered in blood, and dialing 911.

But then why am I here?

His eyes suddenly became heavy. He closed them and was out.

≈∙≋

Rhonda and Ray sat in the hospital coffee shop nursing lattes. "OK, Ray, what's up? What do you need?"

"You always were perceptive."

"I've known you for a long time. I can always tell when there's something you want from me. Like that one time in college when Brian made up his mind to join that dangerous fraternity, and you had me talk him out of it."

Ray smiled. "It's possible that Brian may forget

everything that has happened lately, but it isn't over by any means. He will have to endure extensive therapy and will most likely be put on medication."

Rhonda nodded. "I assumed all that."

"Unfortunately, that won't be enough. He still needs to confront the guilt in his life or he will return to his dark reality."

"What are you asking me to do?"

Ray fingered a napkin on the table. This wasn't easy for him to say. "Help him confront the guilt."

She snorted. "I'm not a psychologist, Ray. You know that. How can I possibly help him?"

"By talking to him. You stress the importance of working through the accident." He sipped his drink. "Tell me—and be honest—have *you* dealt with what happened?"

Rhonda toyed with the plastic lid on her coffee cup. "I guess, as much as I can. It's been hard, but I've learned to cope. And I've spent a lot of time in prayer." She looked up. "But if you're asking me whether or not I forgive him, there's nothing to forgive. It was an accident."

"So, the fact that he was drinking when it happened plays no role in your opinion?"

She didn't answer.

"Look, I only ask because it means something to him. It may very well be the reason he's slipped into such a dreadful psychological state."

"Yes, I was angry that he'd been drinking, but I also know that wasn't why I lost my baby." She stared Ray in the eye, fresh tears brimming over her lids. "We were excited, dancing around like idiots on the landing. What happened could have happened even if he was sober. No one is to blame for that. God took my baby home. I cling to the fact that God protected her somehow. Maybe even from all this madness. I don't know."

"OK, because what I'm asking you to do won't be easy. I don't think he's ready for me to talk to him yet. Eventually, a counselor will be assigned to him, but for now, he trusts you. We *need* you."

"I understand."

Ray pushed back his chair and stood.

"Wait," she said, standing next to him. "I have to know something."

"What's that?"

"Will he be able to go home with me when he heals from the gunshot wound?"

The question he had dreaded. There it was. He didn't meet her gaze. His heart hurt for this woman.

"Ray, please. No more secrets."

He lifted his head and smiled a forced grin. "We'll see."

"Don't hold back anymore. I'm begging you to give it to me straight." Rhonda squared her shoulders and studied his face.

"It's very unlikely that he'll be able to go home with you. He's been diagnosed with a pretty serious condition, and the fact that he tried to commit suicide— "

She cut him off. "But you said he didn't really know he was shooting himself."

"All the more reason they would send him away."

"Send him away?" she choked.

"To Brighton Mental Hospital."

Rhonda's eyes rolled back in her head and her body swayed.

Oh no. Ray leapt at her, just in time to catch her

head before it hit the table. He set her limp body in the chair, and silently scolded himself for being so callous. Couldn't the news have waited? But she had pushed him to be truthful. Ray rested her head on the table and looked around the room.

The woman behind him held a glass of ice water.

"Excuse me," Ray said, "But my friend has passed out. May I borrow your water?"

The woman instantly complied.

"Thank you."

Ray lifted her head, and sprinkled water on Rhonda's face.

She grimaced and blinked twice, before her eyes fluttered open. Instantly, she grabbed her head. "What happened?"

"You fainted," Ray said, returning to his chair. "How do you feel?"

Rhonda rubbed her temples. "A bit of a headache."

"Would you like me to get you some aspirin?"

"Just give me a second. If it doesn't clear, I have some pain pills in my purse."

"I'm sorry about springing it on you like that. You told me to be honest, but I guess I could have been more sensitive in my approach."

She furnished him a half smile. "No, your delivery was fine. I just have a lot to digest."

"Yes, and I'm here if you need more clarified."

Rhonda nodded. "Ray, you've been a true friend. I only wish Brian could see it."

"I'm his scapegoat."

"Yes, and I'm sorry about that."

"It's OK. I believe God will heal our friendship in time."

Rhonda patted his arm. "I'm sure you're right." She stood and motioned toward the door. "I'd better get back." She tossed her cup in the metal container by the door and left for Brian's room.

Ray sighed.

"There you are." Danielle walked to the table carrying a duffel bag. "I brought Rhonda some of my clothes, and stopped by the drug store to pick up some toiletries."

"You're a God-send, Danielle. Thank you."

"I would have been here sooner, but I kind of fell asleep on my couch." Danielle giggled a nervous laugh, and then pushed the bag across the table. "How is Brian doing? Any better?"

"Better? Well, he's out of ICU. So, I guess you could say that. Though he has so many other issues to break through."

Danielle reached out and touched his hand.

Unsure why, Ray recoiled. Instantly, he regretted it.

Her countenance fell. She stared at him, and then stammered, "Um, well, I will be praying for him."

"Yeah. Thank you." A strange, uncomfortable void seemed to plummet in between them. He wanted to fix it, but nothing seemed right, so he remained quiet.

After several seconds of awkward silence, Danielle slid back in the chair and stood. "Well, if you need anything, you've got my number."

"Of course. And thanks for the clothes."

She gave a strained smile, waved, and disappeared into the corridor.

Well, I'm the biggest jerk ever. Here she brings some of her own clothes, stops to get stuff for Rhonda, too, and I treat her like an irritation. Not that he had any clue how this could have gone down any different. When she touched his hand, something in him said, "No, not now." He couldn't explain it. *Lord, why is this so difficult? Sure, this isn't the perfect time to start a relationship, but even letting her be my friend would be good for me.*

He scooted back in his chair and walked to the counter to get a refill. Something said in his heart to run after her. To dial her number this instant and make her come back. But a voice in his head held him back.

Giving in to the second voice, he grabbed his coffee and started the walk back to Brian's recovery room.

అం

Danielle rushed through the lobby in a blur, dashed across the parking lot, and fumbled with her keys. Once inside her car, she let the waterworks flow. How could she be so stupid?

The man didn't love her, he was just being nice. Or maybe he did like her at first, but reality set in. She was an embarrassment.

Did Rhonda know that everyone thought Danielle had had an affair with her husband? Had Rhonda told Ray to stay away from her? Whatever the reason, Ray had blatantly shunned her.

The amber light reflected in the car, and in the eerie silence, Danielle cried. Buckets of tears rested in her lap. Her jeans were wet, and her nose was so clogged, she had to breathe through her mouth. How ridiculous. He's just a man.

Her heart retorted, "A man I'm slowly falling in love with."

৵৽

Brian sat in what looked like a field of dark purple flowers. In the distance, he could see his daughter collecting a bouquet.

"Lara?" he called.

She smiled and started for him, but something made her stop. The young girl's face went deathly pale. She turned and ran away into the forest behind her.

"Lara!" Brian screamed, running toward her. But it was too late, she'd vanished. Brian turned to see what had frightened his little girl away.

A malevolent veil filled the field behind him.

Fear seized Brian's core. Brian shot awake, and almost fell out of bed.

"Honey, are you OK? Should I get the nurse?" Rhonda asked.

His heart thumped wildly. He labored to still his breathing. "No, it's OK. I'm fine," he said. "I just had an awful nightmare."

Rhonda sat back in her chair, not looking fully convinced.

Brian noticed her apprehensive stare. "Really, sweetheart, I'm fine." He laid his right hand on hers and closed his eyes again.

৵৽

Brian worked to open his eyes. A hazy outline of Rhonda's silhouette came into view. "Rhonda," he slurred.

"I'm here. Do you need some water?"

Brian nodded the best he could.

She picked up a small, mustard-colored pitcher by the side of the bed and poured him a glass of water.

Brian tried to sit up, but winced at the sharp pain in his abdomen.

"Wait, let me help you." She lifted his head so he could drink. Some of it spilled out on his gown.

"Brian, we need to talk."

Is she serious? His head throbbed, and all he wanted was to close his eyes and sleep. "Now?"

"Yes, this can't wait." She passed him a towel.

He didn't say anything, but looked at her.

"Brian," she started, "We need to talk about the night Lara died."

His pulse raced. He turned his head to face the wall. A small crack punctured the yellow paint. He fixated on it.

She slid around to the other edge of the bed, blocking the view of his paint crack, and touched his arm. "You need to know that I don't blame you for what happened. It was an accident. Please stop blaming yourself."

"I can't," he mumbled.

"Why not?"

His body trembled. Something seemed to take control of him. He couldn't stop shaking.

"Talk to me, Brian. I need you to tell me why you can't forgive yourself and get past the guilt?"

Tears stained his pillow. "It was my fault."

Rhonda pulled on his shoulder, forcing him to face her. "No, it wasn't. We were dancing on the stairs—a stupid thing to do. Yes. But you can't put the sole responsibility on yourself."

"I was drunk."

"Yes," Rhonda nodded, "and I have to admit I was

mad, at first."

He frowned.

She leaned forward and lifted his chin. With a small smile, she said, "But I don't think that's why it happened. And even if it was, you have to let it go. I've forgiven you. You need to forgive yourself. And you especially need to ask God to forgive you. "

"God?" Brian sneered. "It's God Who did this."

"Oh, so first it's your fault, and now it's God's?"

"Mostly His."

She shook her head. "No, Brian. Did God *allow* it to happen? Maybe. But did He *do* it? No. You have so much guilt wrapped up inside, that it's destroying you. If anyone should be suffering, it should be me. I'm the one who wanted a baby."

"And I didn't?" he snapped.

"You know what I mean."

"Which is why I can't forgive myself. Or God."

Rhonda sighed. "Then you'll never get better. And I need you better. I would like my husband back."

"How can I?" He flipped over on his back and stared at the ceiling.

"You know, Brian, bad things happen to good people because of our sin."

"*My* sin?"

"No, *our* sin; the world's sin. But I like to think that Lara is in heaven playing with the angels. I get excited, because I know that someday I will see her again. But, Brian, I'm sad because I know you won't be joining us. If that bullet had killed you, that would be it for us. I'd never get to introduce you to the child who once lived in my womb." Emotion seemed to clutch her throat, and her voice became raspy. "But I know a way that you can find peace and forgiveness from your guilt. I know a way that someday you can meet your daughter."

Tears cascaded down Brian's cheeks.

"You just need to turn your life over to Jesus. Let go, and let God take care of your sorrow." Rhonda kissed his damp face and whispered, "You need to pour out your heart to the One who can carry your pain."

"I don't think I can."

Rhonda climbed into the narrow bed alongside of him, placed her head on his shoulder and said, "Jesus died and rose again, so that you could live."

Brian shivered. "I'm sorry, but I can't."

26

Ray looked at the address book on his phone. Danielle's name stared at him, daring him to push send. But he couldn't. What would he say? That he was an idiot. All night, when he should have been concentrating on praying and comforting Rhonda, regret clutched his gut.

He squeezed his eyes shut and sighed. Now was not the time. He snapped his phone closed and stuffed it in his coat pocket.

Rhonda had mentioned Brian was awake and free for a visit. That took precedence.

He'd think about Danielle later. Or at least, he'd try to make it later. He stood and walked to Brian's room.

Brian was sitting up.

"Well, you're looking much better." Ray smiled.

"Really? I feel like an armored tank used my stomach as a roadway."

Ray chuckled. "Do you need anything?"

"Actually, I'd love that pillow on the floor next to you," Brian said pointing. "I can't bend at the waist yet, so if it falls, it stays there."

Ray reached for the pillow and put it behind Brian's head. "Look, I know it's been a hard year for us, but I'd really like to work it out. We *were* best friends once and—"

"If we're such good friends, why'd you have to

sell me out? I trusted you and you used me to make yourself look good."

Unbelievable. Ray sat across from him with narrowed his eyes. "Is that what you think happened? That I sold you out?"

"Well, didn't you?"

"No, man. Not at all. When things started getting crazy, I defended you. I even asked Dr. Jai if I could handle your case. I figured if I was involved, I could buy you more time and try to help you come to grips with what was going on. Obviously, I failed you."

Brian seemed to consider this before responding. "What happened to me, Ray? And be straight."

And there it was. Ray took a deep breath before answering. He didn't want to hit Brian the same way he socked Rhonda. "This isn't going to be easy. It may even be hard to believe."

"I doubt anything you say could stun me."

"We believe you may have schizophrenia."

Brian blinked.

"It appears that for several months now, you've been living in a make-believe world."

"Schizophrenia? But how's that possible? I'm almost forty years old. Schizophrenia manifests itself in someone's character in their early twenties."

"I don't know," Ray ran his hand through his hair, "but that's not the only thing that has us baffled."

"What else?" Brian asked, raising his eyebrows.

"Well, your MRI didn't come back conclusive. As I'm sure you know, with schizophrenia the lateral ventricles are enlarged. Though you show all the symptoms outwardly, yours aren't any larger than a normal person's." Ray sat in the chair next to Brian and leaned forward. "You also show symptoms that resemble DID. We're looking into that, too."

"Well, I can't be both."

"Yes, but you're also a human being, not a textbook. We're trying to figure this out. But it could take some time."

"Maybe I'm neither."

Ray shrugged. "I don't know, Brian. You have to be something. You know, as well as I do, that no one shows signs of altered realities without some sort of psychosis." Ray sighed. "But the one thing that we're pretty sure about is *why* it revealed itself."

"Rhonda's accident," Brian said, matter-of-factly.

So, he was talking about the accident. Ray tried not to smile. "Yes, and as you know, schizophrenia is triggered by fear and... "

"What am I afraid of?"

"I don't know. I was hoping you could shed some light on that. I assumed the accident triggered your condition, but I can't explain the fear."

Brian stared at the ceiling.

"The guilt you've harbored shows that you felt responsible for what happened. Maybe you feared what that could mean. Maybe it's just the trauma of the whole thing. We're doctors who work from theories. Like I said, people are not textbooks."

"What was make-believe?" Brian asked.

"As far as I can tell, I would say the personalities of Lara, Jake, and Dr. Raven."

Brian thought for a moment and then asked, "And I told you about all of those people?"

"You mentioned them on occasion, and I saw you talking a few times when you checked out."

Brian struggled to turn on his side. "What have I put my wife through the past year? She must think I'm crazy."

"She didn't know."

"But she knows now, right?"

"Yes," Ray answered.

"So, when did she find out?"

Ray sighed. "After you shot yourself."

Toying with his lip, Brian didn't respond right away. Finally, he asked, "Can I ask who found me?"

"Danielle."

His face went pale. "Is she OK?"

"Yeah." Ray shifted in the chair, debating if he should say what he was thinking. "I have to admit, I thought the two of you were having an affair."

"Danielle and me?" Brian shook his head. "No. I may have flirted a little, but I never had any real intention of doing anything. I think she kind of liked someone else."

Ray tried not to smile. "Well, I know the truth."

"What truth?"

"That you didn't have an affair."

Brian glanced away to the wall.

"What is it?"

Brian didn't look at him. "I did. With a client."

Adrenaline pumped through Ray's veins. He must have heard wrong. "What did you say?"

"I kissed a client."

Ray sat back, stunned. "Who?"

"Krissy Stephens. Jake's girlfriend..." Brian stopped and wrinkled his brow. "How could that be, if Jake wasn't real?"

Relief washed over Ray like a warm blanket. "She must have been just one more way to cope."

"So, basically you're saying I'm nuts."

"Now, Brian, you know better than to put it that

way." Ray smirked. "But in psychological terms, yes."

"Crazier than some of my patients. That's what Dr. Raven said."

Ray's smile faded. "So you remember him?"

"It comes and goes." Brian wiped at the beads of perspiration that lazed on his upper lip. "Kind of like the memory of a bad dream."

"I know there isn't much I can say to comfort you. But I promise you'll be getting some of the best counselors to help you get through this."

Brian sighed. "But I'm done, right? I'll never be on the counseling side of the couch again."

"I don't know. Only time and lots of prayer will tell."

Brian shivered despite the tepid temperature.

"Are you OK?" Ray asked.

"I think I need a drink."

Ray shook his head. "Not going to happen, my friend."

"I know, but I must be having withdrawals."

"How much do you think you drink a day?" Ray wasn't sure he wanted that answer.

His friend pulled the covers to his chin and visibly shivered. "I don't know. Probably a bottle."

"A bottle of what? Of beer or whiskey?"

"The latter. But if you must know, I preferred bourbon." Brian tried to smile, but his teeth chattered.

"For how long?" Ray grabbed an extra blanket from the empty bed, and placed it over him.

"I drank occasionally before. Not that Rhonda ever condoned it. But the downing of bottles...that has been since the accident."

"A bottle a day for six months? You're in for quite a ride."

Brian's head bobbed. "I know."

Ray touched his head. "Do you want me to stay with you until you fall asleep?"

His eyes welled up with tears. "Please," he croaked.

"Then I won't leave you until you're snoring." It hurt to see his friend so broken, but also a sense of peace had begun. A new hope that Brian was seeking help. Ray pushed the button on the bed which allowed Brian's body to move down to the prone position. "Good dreams."

"Right," Brian laughed sarcastically, and allowed his eyes to close.

Ray sat back and watched Brian wrestle for two hours. Finally, his breathing slowed, and Ray breathed again.

❧❦

"What was that?" Brian sat alone in his dimly lit hospital room. Sweat poured down his face, and yet, he couldn't get warm. Every time he closed his eyes, he seemed to hallucinate.

Out of the corner of his eye, he thought he saw something. He turned his head side to side. His skin crawled. *No!* Spiders crawled all over him. Brian threw off the covers, batted at his skin, and scratched madly at his face, until it stung. He pushed the call button several times frantically.

The nurse flipped on the overhead light. "What's wrong, Dr. Manifold?"

Brian looked up at her, panic-stricken. "Kill them!"

She glanced around the room nervously. "I'm sorry, what did you say, sir?"

"The spiders. Kill them, please!"

The nurse grabbed his chart from the door and cautiously approached with the clipboard held high over her head. She searched all around his bed, before responding. "I don't see anything."

"But they're everywhere."

The nurse glanced at the chart in her hand. "Oh." She nodded. "I think you're just experiencing the effects of alcohol withdrawal. Just try to relax, OK? I promise you. There aren't any spiders in here."

A furry creature rushed by his leg. How could he relax? "Can you give me something, please? I can't sleep with insects crawling all over me." He hit his neck, and then scratched at his arm.

The nurse shook her head. "I can't give you anything, but the doctor will be doing his rounds in half an hour. I'll have him stop by. OK?"

"Thank you," Brian said, weakly.

She turned off the light, closed the door and left Brian to contend with his hairy, impalpable friends.

☙❧

Danielle tossed around in her bed for hours. She opened her eyes for the umpteenth time. It was hopeless. She knew her body needed sleep, but her brain was vigilant. She couldn't relax. Her heart was heavy for the Manifolds.

When Brian was catatonic, Rhonda probably thought it was only temporary. This current dilemma was far from temporary. Hours talking with Rhonda broke Danielle's heart. First, Rhonda lost her child. Now her husband would be institutionalized. How would she survive?

A knock at the door made Danielle's heart skip a beat. She glanced at the clock. Who would be here at this hour? Pulling on a robe, she looked through the peephole.

Rhonda.

Danielle unlocked the lock and chain, and opened the door. "Hello. Come on in."

Rhonda offered a wan smile. "I'm sorry to bother you, but I couldn't sleep. Can I come in?"

"I couldn't sleep, either." She stepped back and allowed Rhonda to enter her small apartment. "Would you like some herbal tea? I have a few flavors."

"That would be lovely," Rhonda said.

They went into the kitchen, and Danielle put on a kettle of water.

"Thank you for the clothes."

Danielle waved a hand in the air. "No worries."

"Do you like chai?"

"Love it," Rhonda said, pulling off her sweater. "I know you're probably wondering why I'm here, in your home, in the middle of the night."

"I can guess." Danielle grinned, set two teacups on the counter, and then went for the box of sweetener.

"This is going to sound crazy, but God told me to. He said there is something you're supposed to tell me." Rhonda pinched her lips together, letting her gaze drop to the counter.

It took only a moment for the answer to come to Danielle. "For the past month, I've been waking up in the middle of the night to some intense dreams. A sort of urgency to pray. I never knew for whom, or the reason. I just knew I was supposed to pray." The teapot whistled, and she turned off the stove and poured water over the bags resting in the china bottoms.

"Go on," Rhonda urged.

"Then tonight, I had the familiar stirring, only this time it was different. This time I saw your face. I was supposed to pray for you."

Rhonda stopped mid-sip, and stared at her new friend.

"I know that's odd. I hardly know you. But our God knows both us, and He knows our needs. The same Spirit Whom you asked for help, came to me in my sleep and asked me to pray."

"Thank you." Rhonda began to softly cry.

Danielle reached across the counter and touched her hand. "I promise to continue to pray, if you promise to not give up."

Rhonda nodded.

The two women, practically strangers, hugged. It was as if they had known each other for years.

27

The first time it was spiders, and then ghosts. Now, Brian wasn't sure what they were. He closed his eyes in an attempt to block them out, but they were there, too. He couldn't stop shaking. He'd asked for something to help him sleep several times, but they hadn't come yet.

A psychiatrist had seen him earlier to evaluate his condition and Brian assumed the man had told the staff to let Brian sweat out the withdrawals. He couldn't be angry, because he might have done the same thing.

"I can't do this!" Brian yelled at the dark.

"I told you," a voice said from a gloomy shadow in his room.

Working to clear the sweat dripping into his eyes, Brian squinted, but saw nothing. "Who's there?"

Silence.

"Come on. I've got enough problems. Just tell me who you are?"

Silence.

Brian frantically pushed the nurse's call button. The sound of feet clomped down the corridor.

Brian sighed with relief when the door opened.

A different nurse than before flipped on the overhead light.

Brian glanced at her, and then back to the corner. Nothing.

"What's wrong, sir?"

Brian continued to watch the corner. Where could it have gone? What had goaded him?

"Sir?"

He glanced at the woman, not really wanting to look away from the corner. "Can you leave the light on?" he asked.

The nurse glanced at the corner suspiciously. "Sure," she replied. "Is that all?"

"Can I have something to knock me out? I asked earlier and the nurse said a half hour. It's been at least two hours." His voice shook, as he added, "I really need it."

"Let me check with the doctor. I'll be right back."

The nurse left, and Brian stared back at the corner. "I know you're there, coward." He studied the room.

In the corner sat a mauve metal chair and a small gray trashcan. To his left a TV, a shelf, and to the right, a window and a bathroom door. Even though the room appeared empty, he wasn't convinced. Voices still echoed in his mind.

Ray had said that Brian was possibly schizophrenic and if Ray was right, then it could be assumed that Brian would hear voices. He would also hallucinate. Not to mention, Brian was in detox.

The soft patter of the nurse's shoes approached his room.

The thought comforted him.

She entered with a white pill cup and a glass of water. "Here, take these."

Brian's hand trembled as he brought the glass to his mouth. Some water spilt out, but he managed to get the small, pink pills down his throat. "Thank you."

"You're welcome. Now, I hope you can sleep." She

turned to go.

"Wait."

"Yes, Dr. Manifold?"

"Do you have to go?"

She stared at him for a moment, before answering. "I'm sorry, sir, but I have to make some rounds."

"Yes, of course. I'm sorry. I'm just having a hard time adjusting."

"I understand. I'll come back and check on you in a few minutes. But hopefully, those pills will have kicked in by then."

Brian nodded.

"Do you still want me to leave the light on?"

"Yes, please."

She nodded and closed the door.

Alone again.

Brian looked around the room, relieved that his eyes felt heavy.

∂∽∾

"I told you." A voice echoed in the night air.

Where am I?

Brian peered out into the darkness. The only light reflected from the moon. The hypnotic sound of waves could be heard in the distance. The wind smelled of salt and sea. *The ocean.* "Why am I here?" Brian yelled into the night.

The beast cackled. "In order that you understand that you can't get rid of me. I'm always with you." The beast hissed and his glowing red eyes beamed in the dark. "Did you forget me, Brian?"

"No."

"I think you did. You didn't tell them about me,

did you?"

"No."

The beast slithered and clawed at the sand. "Why did you forget me, Brian?"

"I just told you. I didn't."

The beast laughed a vile chuckle that sounded more like a metal sharpener than a laugh. "You really are pathetic. You can't get well. You know that, don't you?"

"I *want* to. That is half the battle."

"No, Brian. You're mine."

"I'm nobody's. You're simply a hallucination. Once I get this craving for alcohol out of my system, you'll be gone forever."

The beast howled, causing the ground around him to shake.

Brian fell to the sand. "What's so funny?"

"You still don't understand our relationship, do you, Brian?"

"I just told you. You're not real."

"Oh, I'm real."

❧❦

The next morning, Danielle drove Rhonda to the hospital. She considered not staying, wanting desperately to avoid Ray. But Rhonda insisted she come in. Her new friend needed her, and Danielle couldn't resist being wanted. Danielle walked down the sterile white hall to the waiting room.

Rhonda stopped at the nurse's station to talk to someone.

Danielle found a seat. A pile of magazines rested a foot away on a round end table. Danielle leaned over and thumbed through the stack. Cars, gardening, and fashion. Nothing looked appealing.

Ray came out of Brian's room.

Her heart accelerated. She grabbed the first magazine she could, and lifted it to her face. *If I can't see him, he can't see me.* An old thing her cousin used to say when they were little. Not that it was true, but right now, she hoped it helped.

"I never would have taken you to be a biker girl," Ray said.

Shoot! Danielle grimaced, lowered the magazine and frowned. "What?"

Ray pointed to the publication in her hand. "Quite the interesting choice of reading material."

She rolled her eyes and tossed the periodical aside. "I'm bored. What can I say?"

He stared at her, amused. "I see."

Danielle wasn't in the mood for this; maybe yesterday she'd been flattered, but not now. This second, she just wanted him to keep walking. She crossed her arms, kicked out her legs, and stared at the TV across the room.

Ray didn't leave.

Go away. His very presence unnerved her.

He sat next to her and his cologne filled her nose. Why couldn't he stink? She tried to block out the pulse in her neck that pounded in her ears. Though her gaze focused on an old rerun, her heart was solely centered on him.

"Did you get any sleep last night?" he asked.

"A little." Her chest heaved and she hoped he didn't notice how she felt.

"Me, either."

They both stared straight ahead.

If he was anything like her, there was no denying the chemistry flowing between them. The elephant in the room needed to be squashed.

How she wanted to blurt out what a jerk he was being. That she really cared about him.

That they needed to kiss quickly before a phone call or another tragedy occurred.

She did nothing. She stayed focused on someone making a joke about a teddy bear.

❧

The early morning sunlight poured into his room. Brian slowly opened his eyes. He couldn't believe it. He'd actually managed to sleep through part of the night.

"Good morning."

Relief. It was Rhonda.

"You're a sight for sore eyes," he said.

Rhonda leaned over and kissed him. "I think you'll be released soon, but I need to talk to your doctor to find out for sure."

"I'm going home?"

Rhonda looked away.

His heart sank. "No," he said, dryly. "I'm going to the nut house."

She faced him with a forced smile. "Ray set you up with a good friend of his. He told me you're doing much better, so maybe it won't be for long. You've come through the withdrawals and you haven't been hallucinating, lately. So, I'm sure you'll be home in no time." Her mock cheerfulness rubbed like broken cement.

Brian couldn't tell her about the beast. He couldn't

let her know that he still wasn't alone. That the disorder still guided his reality. He pinched his lips together in what he hoped resembled a smile. "I'm sure you're right."

"Well, visiting hours are almost up and I need to speak to your doctor, so I'd better get going. I'll see you in the morning, OK?"

Brian kissed her. Her lips were warm and inviting. How long had it been since he had held his wife? He missed her. And it appeared he would go on missing her.

28

Danielle stretched her legs out in front of the swing and allowed gravity to rock her forward.

Ray stood at the edge of the swing set, holding one of the metal legs. Why they'd ended up in a park, she wasn't sure, but it was empty—the perfect place to finally talk.

"You want me to push you," he teased.

She shook her head. "Not on your life."

He held up his hands in mock surrender. "OK, OK. Just checking."

A slight breeze blew, ruffling her hair. She pushed it back out of her face, and looked at Ray.

His expression was odd. Confusing. What did he want from her? Right now, he seemed interested. Yesterday, repulsed.

"So, you got me here. Talk," she said, a bit more abruptly than she meant to.

He laughed nervously. "I, um, know that there has been some tension between us. Sometimes good, other times—"

"Bad."

He frowned, and walked to the other swing. "Yeah."

"To be honest, I don't understand any of it. If you don't want a relationship with me, just say so."

"I know it seems that way—"

Danielle stopped swinging and glanced at him.

His strong jaw appeared tense, his eyes lost.

"You are the most confusing man I've ever met. Do you like me or not? I'm a big girl, just tell me."

He crossed in front of her, grabbed the chains above her head and pulled her face only inches from his.

For a second, her heart stopped. She wanted to grab the back of his head and kiss him. His gaze sought hers. Why couldn't he just let go? "Just tell me," she repeated in a whisper.

"When the time is right, and the madness stops, I want you in my life for good."

❧❦

Brian dropped his toothbrush into his small travel bag.

Rhonda yelled to the bathroom door, "Are you ready, dear?"

"I'll be out in a second." He stared at his reflection, his eyes dark and puffy, his cheeks hollow and gray. He hardly recognized himself. But it wasn't his appearance that bothered him. It was the future closing in. Perspiration on his upper lip was the only true tell of how he felt at the moment.

He squeezed his eyes shut and tried to remember a happier time. Anything that could bring peace to this angst, this pyre that burned inside. Suffocating him. Keeping him from being the man who used to look at him in the mirror. He grabbed his bag and stepped back into the room.

Rhonda was doing a final sweep, visually checking nooks and crannies, bed, drawers, countertops. "Ready?" she asked.

How did one get ready for this? To hide the truth that was sure to be in his gaze, he glanced down at his jeans and T-shirt, then to his right hand that held a cherry-wood cane. "As ready as a crippled man can be."

"You're not crippled," she smiled, "just full of holes."

"Very funny." He hobbled over to her and caressed her cheek with the back of his fingers. "I do love you. You know that?"

"Absolutely. You have to."

"And why is that, Mrs. Manifold?"

Rhonda placed her forehead against his. "Because you're stuck with me."

He lifted her chin and kissed her tenderly. He withdrew and sat on the bed.

"Brian?" Rhonda joined him.

"I'm scared," he said with a shudder.

"God will take care of you," Rhonda answered. "I know you don't believe in Him, but I do."

"I wish I had your faith."

"I wish you did, too."

A male orderly rapped on the door before entering with a wheel chair. "The van has arrived," he said. "Are you ready to go, sir?"

Brian shot Rhonda one more desperate look. The concern in her eyes broke his heart.

Rhonda looked away and nodded to the man.

The man helped Brian stand and hobble to the metal chair.

A white van waited just outside the door.

Rhonda stepped to his side and kissed him one last time.

The orderly helped him into the van and passed

him his bag.

Rhonda's gaze met his through the van window and his heart broke into smaller pieces. Would he ever see his wife again?

∂∽⽥

The van pulled up to an iron gate, and the driver rolled down his window to flash a badge to the guard.

The guard stepped back in the vertical shack and the heavy gate slid open.

Lush trees adorned the immaculate lawns. A small cobblestone path followed the extent of the property. Tall pillars lined each side of the three-story brick building.

"Where is everyone?" Brian asked the driver.

The driver wheeled the van into an S-shaped driveway, turned off the ignition and faced him. "Aren't you supposed to be a psychiatrist?"

"Psychologist."

"What's the difference?"

"More schooling. A psychiatrist is an M.D. They can prescribe medication. A psychologist cannot."

"OK, either way. Haven't you brought anyone here before?"

Brian shook his head.

"Well, this isn't a country club, my friend. Patients aren't allowed outside."

Brian's heart dropped into his aching stomach. He scanned the building, and this time he noticed barred windows.

The driver stepped outside the vehicle and walked around to Brian's side. "Welcome to your new home, Doctor."

Inside he cringed. How would he make it here? Brian grabbed his cane and the man helped him down. The driver then grabbed the suitcase and motioned for Brian to follow him up the stairs. Brian was relieved to reach the last step.

They entered through a pair of double white doors, to a glass-enclosed reception area.

The driver stepped to the desk and passed a clipboard through a security slot.

The door to the right of the lobby buzzed.

The driver turned to Brian. "OK, you're all theirs."

A nurse came around the counter to hand the driver his clipboard, and then waved for Brian to join her.

Brian stepped inside, and the metal door slammed with a bang behind them. He jumped.

"This way, Dr. Manifold."

He turned back to the nurse and followed her through two more security doors before reaching a waiting area. At the end of the white, sterile room sat a small desk. A nurse sat in a chair, staring at a monitor, while typing on a computer keyboard.

The room resembled something out of a sci-fi space movie. Everything was white and plastic. A strong odor of ammonia mixed with cafeteria food filled his nostrils. His stomach turned.

"All right, I need you to sign here," the nurse said, handing him a clipboard with paperwork and pen.

"What am I signing?"

"Your rights away," she answered matter-of-factly.

He stopped the pen mid-air. "I'm sorry?"

"You have walked in of your own accord. Therefore, you sign over your care to us. If your wife brought you in, then she would sign. If a medical doctor brought you to us, he'd sign. But since you came willingly, you must sign."

"I understand that. What I don't understand is giving up my rights."

"It's simple, Doctor," she said sternly. "We need your permission to help you. In order to do that, we must be able to tell you what to do. When we feel you're ready, we will release you. At that time, you regain your rights. Is that clear?"

"Yes, it's clear. Just a bit scary."

"I understand."

Brian's hand shook as he scribbled his name on the bottom line. He didn't know what he was getting himself into. He knew he needed help, but he also knew he liked being in control. He only hoped that he was in the best care. He handed her the clipboard.

"Now, I will need to see your things."

"Why?"

She frowned. "I can see you're going to be a troublemaker."

"I'm a psychologist. I'm used to asking questions." He smiled, hoping she'd take the joke well. He failed.

"We need to make sure you aren't bringing in anything that could be detrimental to your state of wellbeing. I will look through your things, and then return them to your room later." She leaned over and pushed a button on an intercom. "Nate, the patient for room 266 is ready." She turned back to Brian as the door buzzed behind her. "Nate is the orderly for your floor. You can go with him now."

The orderly didn't look human. His hairy arms were round like watermelons, and he was nearly two feet taller.

Brian didn't wait for Nate to get him.

The door slammed behind them. He jumped again.

"A little jumpy, aren't you?" Nate taunted.

Brian didn't respond. He didn't dare. This goon could flatten him with one flick of a little finger.

They stepped down a corridor filled with white metal doors, each with a small slit at the top.

Nate stopped at an open door at the end of the hall. "Home, sweet home." Nate motioned for Brian to enter.

Brian slowly approached the dim, florescent lit room. Inside sat a mattress covered by a cream blanket, a small nightstand supporting a gold Gideon Bible, and a door that Brian assumed must be a bathroom.

When he stepped inside, Nate closed the door behind him.

The keys jingled in the lock on the outside, and then footsteps echoed away down the hall.

Brian allowed his body to slump to the floor. His chest constricted, and he thought he might hyperventilate. Pulling out a trick he used on patients, he began counting backwards, starting with ten. "Ten," he breathed. "Nine. Eight. Seven. Six." By five, he felt better. He closed his eyes and allowed his body to crumple the rest of the way to the tile. The floor felt ice cold. He rolled over onto his stomach and crawled like a dog to the mattress.

Why is this happening to me?

Maybe the beast was right. He'd reached hell.

29

"Amen," Danielle said.

"Amen," Rhonda echoed, and then wiped tears from her cheeks.

They'd just spent an hour in prayer, something they now did every day after Danielle left work. Never had she felt so close to someone, not even her mother. God had brought them together for a purpose, and Danielle valued their friendship.

"All that praying made me hungry." Rhonda unfolded her legs from the floor and stood. "I have leftover vegetable lasagna the church brought over, or chocolate crunch cake."

Danielle grinned.

"Cake, it is," Rhonda said, smiling back. She walked in the kitchen and pulled down a pair of china plates. They clanked as she placed them on the counter. Then she slid a foil-covered glass pan in between them, uncovered it, and retrieved a knife from the drainer by the sink.

The smell of chocolate wafted in the air. *Comfort to my psyche.* The cake was covered in what looked like fudge frosting and pecans, and a ribbon of caramel ran in waves around the outside.

"Don't even think of saying, 'Just a small piece,'" Rhonda said. "I have no intention of divulging in this sin without a partner. The church keeps bringing me stuff."

Danielle laughed. "Oh, no problem there. I'll take a big piece. That looks amazing."

Rhonda cut a block-size slice and slapped it on a plate.

Danielle picked up her fork, slid it into the dessert, and then brought it to her mouth. "Mmm, how can you call this sin? It's heavenly."

"So, now that we are eating comfort food—"

"Yes?" Danielle eyed her new friend suspiciously.

"Tell me about Ray."

Danielle dropped her fork to the plate. "Aah! Do I have to?"

Rhonda laughed. "You don't think I'm feeding you cake for nothing. Call it a bribe. I want details."

"That man is so frustrating. I don't understand him at all."

"Explain it to me. I've known him forever. Maybe I can help."

A vision of him almost kissing her in the park made her pause. "One minute, he seems totally interested. The next, extremely unapproachable. I don't know who he is really, or what he wants. I'm not even sure my heart cares anymore."

Rhonda stared at her with an amused grin.

"What?"

"I've known Ray for almost twenty years. He's never looked at another woman the way he looks at you."

Whatever. Danielle crossed her arms and sat back on the stool. "OK, then. Explain the lack of commitment. The fickle nature of his gestures."

"Simple—Brian."

Instantly, Danielle felt guilty. It was the obvious reason. One she knew. "I'm sorry, Rhonda. I must sound totally insensitive."

Rhonda waved her off. "Don't be silly. Even if all Brian's problems were simple, Ray would still be there. He has a sickness, an older brother complex with Brian."

"I thought they were the same age."

Rhonda smiled. "They are. But you wouldn't know it by their relationship. It's always been that way. Ray looks out for Brian. For most of their friendship, Brian valued it. He wouldn't do anything without calling Ray first. Then things changed."

"The accident?"

"Yeah. For some reason, Brian didn't want to hear from Ray anymore. Cut him totally out of his life. But then, he did the same to me." Rhonda licked some frosting from her fork and sighed.

A nagging question wouldn't let go, she had to ask. "Be honest with me."

"About what?"

"Can Ray be intimate with a woman, or am I wasting my time."

Rhonda raised an eyebrow. "Intimate?"

Danielle blew through her lips. "Not physically, of course. I mean emotionally. Can he let go of Brian a little and love a woman?"

"Love you?"

Adrenaline shot through her heart to her stomach. "I suppose," Danielle said. "Yeah."

The answer didn't come quickly. Rhonda stared at her plate, way longer than Danielle could stand. Her lack of an answer was scary.

Danielle started to worry.

"I think if you're the right woman, Ray will take that chance. He's just a bit shy when it comes to girls.

You just have to be patient."

Patient? Danielle shoved another bite of cake in her mouth, not sure she was happy with that answer. *God, if Ray is the right one, please make it sooner, rather than later.*

❧

"Good morning, Brian."

Brian squinted. A bald man in a white doctor's jacket and a big smile came into focus.

"I'm Dr. James Coulson. I will be your therapist while you're here with us at Brighton Hospital. Are you hungry?"

Brian sat up and nodded.

"Great, it's lunch time. Come with me."

"Lunch time?"

"I'm afraid you overslept the breakfast hour. But you're just in time for lunch." Brian followed him to a cafeteria line.

James handed him a red plastic tray and said, "Don't get used to sleeping in around here though. From now on, the orderlies will be in to fetch you first thing in the morning. It's their job to make sure everyone consumes three meals a day. It's the only way we can make sure those with eating disorders, and those trying to starve themselves, eat."

A rather large Asian woman scooped a brown, soupy mixture onto Brian's plate, along with soggy carrots and a rock-like biscuit.

"You eat here on purpose?" Brian asked, as they passed him his plate.

"Only on my patient's first day. After that, I bring a bagged lunch."

"Good to know they gave me a smart counselor."

James smiled and led Brian to a small table by some windows in the corner.

Brian looked outside. He could make out a few trees through the black bars.

"I count myself lucky that Ray recommended that the board appoint me to be your counselor. It's not every day that one of our own comes to join us. It makes research all the more interesting. You can explain your situation better than any other client. I'm excited to observe your progress."

Brian toyed with the brown goop on his plate. "I hope you realize, Doctor, that I'm not just some rat in your lab."

The doctor stopped mid-bite. "Of course not. I didn't mean it like that. I just meant that you're an interesting case, and I look forward to helping you. Believe it or not, no one else bartered to help you. After all, you're intelligent, and know the tricks of the trade. Though it may be intriguing, it will also be more difficult."

"I'm here to get well."

"And that's our goal."

❧❦

Brian reclined on a leather sofa in Dr. Coulson's office. The thought was unnerving. He belonged on the other side of the couch, not here.

James sat across from him and started to count backwards in a soothing pitch.

"Brian, I want you to listen to my voice. Eight. As I count, I want you to sense your body. Seven. How heavy it seems. Six. Now relax each muscle. Five. Feel them sinking into the couch. Four. Slowly, begin to relax. Three. You should feel nothing. Two. One."

Brian was out.

"So, you've returned?"

Brian knew that voice. He looked around. *Where am I?* It appeared to be an alley of some kind. He'd been here before. He glanced ahead to a streetlight. The tawny moon cast an eerie glow and Brian could see his surroundings.

To his right were over a dozen overflowing garbage cans and empty boxes. To his left was a metal staircase that led to a four-story apartment window above. The beast lingered ahead of him, just beyond an old fashion lamppost.

Brian set out in the direction of the light.

"Did you miss me?"

"No!" Brian screamed and burst into a run.

"I think you did. You and I, we're one."

Brian skidded to a stop. "Never!"

The beast circled the light, and the bulb popped. Brian stumbled in the sudden darkness and plummeted to his knees.

"Oh, Brian. You can never be free. This is such a waste of time."

"What is?" Using the post, Brian pulled himself up. "What's a waste of time? Fighting for my life? I'm not drinking anymore. I've accepted what happened. Why are you still here?"

The beast leaned in to him.

Brian winced at the fowl stench of the creature's breath. "Do you not know where you are?"

Brian skimmed his surroundings in the moonlit sky. "San Diego, the Gaslamp Quarter, I think."

The beast wrapped his claw around Brian's throat

and squeezed.

Brian gasped for air.

It squeezed until Brian thought his eyes would rupture.

Out of the blue, the creature let go.

Brian grasped at his throat and heaved air. "Why did you do that?" Brian rasped.

"You inconsequential fool. How much longer do I have to put up with you? You never left the good doctor's couch. They seek your illness—a disorder that they'll write down, but will never find. You see, Brian, you can't be cured. You're mine."

❧

It felt like paperweights sat on each of Brian's eyelids. He blinked, forcing them open. When he tried to lift his arm, it didn't budge. *Not again.* He turned his neck to his side. His arms were bound to the bed. He shook his arms in a vain effort to free himself. Sweat poured down his forehead and ran into his eyes. He tried to wipe it with his shoulder but couldn't reach it. He panicked. His heart raced and his chest heaved. He screamed.

Two new orderlies rushed into the room.

Nate followed.

"Be quiet, Brian," ordered Nate. "Or we'll have to drug you again."

"Please," Brian pleaded. "Don't you get it? I'm claustrophobic. Please untie me."

"I'm sorry, but we have our orders."

"Who gave them?" Brian asked.

"Dr. Coulson."

"Then please get him. I can't stay like this." Brian

wheezed. In his mind, the room rotated. He blinked rapidly to stay focused. "Please, I'll go insane."

Nate snorted. "You'll *go* insane? Good one." He shook his head and turned to the smaller orderly. "Get Dr. Coulson. Tell him, Brian Manifold is awake."

"Yes, sir." The man walked out the door, and shut it.

So, Nate was in charge of the orderlies. Not that it mattered. Brian worked to slow his breathing. In and out. Open. Close. He continued to blink his eyelids, compelling them to clear.

James entered abruptly. "How is he?"

"I think he's having an anxiety attack," Nate answered.

James crossed to Brian.

Brian struggled to look him in the eye.

"Try to look at me," Dr. Coulson said in a soothing voice. "How many fingers am I holding up?"

He felt crossed-eyed. To him, it looked like three, but since the middle one looked blurry, Brian said, "Two."

"Good." James pulled out a skinny silver flashlight and shined it in both of his eyes.

He squinted.

"OK, I need you to breath slower," James said. "If you want me to take the restraints off, you'll have to prove to me that you won't be harmful to me or yourself."

Brian nodded. In. Out. He listened to the sound of his own breath.

"You're not dying. Your heart is racing because of the adrenaline in your body. You need to relax. Think of a babbling brook. Do you see it, doctor?"

Brian closed his eyes.

"Do you see the stream trickling over stones, the lapping sound of water as it rolls by?"

His muscles relaxed.

"The wind blows, soft and warm."

A stream from his childhood appeared in his mind's eye. Smooth pebbles lined the bottom, the water so clear he could see a rainbow of stones.

"Put your hand in the water," James said.

Brian visualized his hand touching the water. It felt cool to the touch. It soothed his skin like silk. The soft sound of the waves lapping against the shore soothed his mind. It was working. Brian opened his eyes.

James stood over him with a big grin plastered on his face. "Now, how do you feel?"

"Better," Brian said.

"Good. Let's get those straps off you so you can join me for dinner."

The two orderlies from before untied his straps and helped him sit up. "Now, Brian, these two will stay with us through our meal. If at any moment they feel I'm threatened, they will put you back in these bonds, do you understand?"

He nodded. *Whatever I did, it must have been bad.* He followed the doctor to the cafeteria, but this time, as promised, James produced a brown paper bag. "I'll wait for you over there. Go ahead, get in line and get yourself some food."

Brian walked behind the last person and acquired a tray. The men around him emerged like zombies. *The dead coming to eat,* thought Brian. *Maybe there's something in the food.*

The cafeteria worker slapped watery potatoes, parched nuggets, and sodden beans onto his plate.

His theory looked more plausible. He grabbed his tray and weaved around the tables, through the dining room, toward James. Brian really didn't feel like eating. And it wasn't even the food; it was the pain in the pit of his stomach. What did he do?

He didn't even remember entering room 266. The last thing he remembered was going to see James earlier in the morning. Brian sat across from his counselor and took a drink of milk. "Can I ask you something?"

"I usually ask the questions, but in this situation I'll allow it." James smiled. Apparently, he must be joking. A little shrink wit.

Unfortunately, Brian had somehow lost his sense of humor. "So, what did I do that made you restrain me?"

James bit into what looked like an egg salad sandwich on wheat bread, and then spoke with a mouth full. "Well, I'm not sure how to answer that."

"You strapped me down. I must have done something awful."

The doctor placed his sandwich on a plastic baggie and took a drink of his soda, before answering. "I don't know that *you* did anything."

Brian stared at James, considering what he just heard. Scared to ask, but scared not to. "So, then, my personalities manifested?"

James gazed out the window and sighed. "I wish I knew. The behavior you implemented today was like none I've ever seen before. And I've seen a lot in the last three decades, I assure you." He looked back at Brian. "It was almost like someone or something controlled you. As if some sort of beast was trying to get out of you."

Brian cringed.

"What is it?"

Sharp pains stabbed Brian in the abdomen. He looked down at his food and his stomach turned. He tried to put his hand to his mouth, but wasn't fast enough. His stomach wretched and he vomited on his tray.

James jumped back and looked to the orderlies.

They ran over and grabbed Brian.

Brian jerked his arms and legs to push them off.

The orderlies managed to grab him and push him to the floor.

Brian turned his face on the cold tile to face James. "I can help you. Please, don't lock me up again."

30

For the fourth time that week, Danielle stopped by Rhonda's house with a box of doughnuts.

"Good morning, Danielle," Rhonda said as she let her in, and then pointed to a slightly plump African-American woman with fire-red hair. "This is my neighbor Melody Brown."

"Hello," Danielle said, smiling.

"Hi," Melody grinned.

Rhonda closed the door. "I need to change. Why don't the two you get acquainted, and I'll be right back."

Danielle waited until Rhonda was out of earshot, before asking, "How's she doing?"

"Not that great, from what I can tell." Melody gave some extent of a smile, and then picked at a maple bar.

"Has she talked to the hospital at all?"

Rhonda entered. "Let's change the subject, OK? I invited you all over here to get my mind off things."

"OK." Danielle reached for a glazed twist and unraveled it. "What shall we talk about?"

"You and Ray," Melody said.

Danielle almost choked on the bite in her mouth. "I'm swarry?" she stuttered, her tongue tangled in the food.

"Come on, juicy details. Inquiring minds want to know." Melody popped a doughnut hole in her mouth and smiled.

"Know what?" Danielle glanced at Rhonda. How did this perfect stranger know about her and Ray? She set her doughnut down and attempted to wipe the sticky frosting from her hands.

Rhonda laughed. "You'll have to excuse my friend, Danielle. Melody has an uncanny way of knowing everybody's business."

"I've been pulling for Ray for years," Melody said, crossing her arms. "I may be an old married woman, but I know when he likes someone."

"When have you seen him?"

"I'm around."

Danielle raised an eyebrow. *Great, a nosy neighbor.* Well, it didn't matter. The timing wasn't right for her and Ray.

"I thought maybe things might have changed," Rhonda said.

"Honestly, I haven't seen him since the last time you and I talked. We're waiting."

"Waiting?" Melody dipped her eyebrows in a confused expression. "I'm sorry. Waiting for what, exactly? The big earthquake? The rapture? World peace?"

Danielle sipped her coffee. *Waiting for what exactly?* The same question ran through her mind daily. Hour by hour. Minute by minute. "I suppose, for Rhonda's hubby to get well."

Melody stared at her a moment, eyes wide. "You're kidding, right?"

I wish I was. Danielle shook her head. "His choice, not mine."

"So, let me get this straight." Melody licked her pink glossed lips. "My good friend, Ray, has put you on hold until Rhonda's husband is better?"

"Apparently."

"Ha!" Melody dropped her doughnut and reached for her purse. She opened the pocket on the side and withdrew a cell phone.

"What are you doing?"

"Getting ready to kick some sense into my pal."

"No!" Danielle practically leapt at Melody, knocking the cell out of her hand. The silver phone slid across the counter, stopping at the edge of Danielle's coffee. "Rhonda, do something."

"You can't call him," Rhonda said.

"Why not?" Melody reached for her phone again. "He's being stupid."

Danielle covered Melody's hand. "Please. I don't want him to hate me. Things have been strained, as it is. If he isn't ready to be more than friends with me, then I'll have to deal with that."

"Hmm..." Melody stared Danielle in the eye, obviously not convinced.

"Please." Danielle forced a smile.

Rhonda nodded. "She's right, Mel."

Melody bit the side of her bottom lip and sighed. "Fine. But if he is still being a jerk a few weeks from now, I'm going let him have it."

Danielle laughed nervously. "Deal."

∂∘∾

Brian sat back on the couch, once again feeling very uneasy about his position. He, a therapist, was now the patient. At least with Dr. Raven, though imaginary, he felt in control. At this point, Brian sat utterly at the mercy of another mind.

James took a seat across from him and crossed his arms. "I'm not going to attempt to hypnotize you again. I'm intrigued by what you have to say in your defense. I think there may be more to your case than the length of my clinical knowledge." He reached for his coffee and continued, "When you lost your lunch, so to speak, something set you off. What was it?"

"Apparently, my colleague knew about the multiple personalities I exhibited, but I never told him about my recurring dreams."

The doctor raised an eyebrow. "Your dreams?"

"Yes, I have a recurring visitor. I'm usually not in the same place more than once." Brian stopped and rolled his eyes. "Well, once I was, but usually I'm not."

James nodded.

"You said his name at lunch and that is when I lost it."

"I did?"

"Yes, I call him the *beast*." Brian trembled, his eyes rolled back.

James came out of his chair. "Are you OK?"

He inhaled deeply, trying to get his bearings. "I think so, but I think there is something very real about my dreams. They haunt me, even when I'm awake. They feel more like a hallucination than Lara, Jake, or Raven did, but somehow more real, too." He paused. "Then again, I wonder if they're all connected in some strange way."

"Is there any kind of message given by this beast in your dreams?"

"He constantly tells me that I'm his."

"His? The beast's?"

Brian shuddered. "Yes."

James paced for about ten minutes, scratched his

head one minute and his chin the next.

The moving target began to make Brian dizzy.

"Dr. Manifold, I'll be back." Dr. Coulson finally spoke. "Can I trust you to be OK while I'm gone?"

"I'll be fine. I promise."

His therapist stepped out into the hall and closed the door.

Brian took the chance to glance around the man's office. It reminded him of his own office at St. Ruth's. The walls were brown and green and the desk, mahogany wood. The tempered windows had a view into the corridor.

Through the glass door, Dr. Coulson made a phone call at the nurses' station.

❧

Ray switched the phone receiver from one hand to the other, trying to understand what he'd just heard. "You can't be serious, James."

"I know this all sounds insane, but honestly, I don't know how else to explain it," James said.

Ray's father, Floyd, had been James Coulson's friend for years. When Ray heard that Brian would be admitted to a mental hospital, he pushed for Brian to be under James's care. Ray trusted him. He knew James would call him when he knew something. Ray just didn't expect *this*.

"What do you want me to do?"

Silence.

"James?"

"Sorry, it's just that I don't know. I've never encountered this before. I know schizophrenia, Ray. I see it all the time, but I'm telling you, what I experienced today is something else. You have to help me out. Bring your dad in on this."

"I'll call him tonight and get back to you in the morning," Ray said. "How's he doing now?"

"He's fine, but exhausted. I need to figure this out so I can start treating him."

Ray grieved. In some weird way, he felt like what happened to Brian was happening to him. "So, you're sure it isn't schizophrenia or DID?"

"I'm not convinced of anything yet, but I do know this case is far from conventional."

"So, the meds aren't working?"

"They didn't even faze him."

"It's only been a couple of days. Maybe we should give it more time."

"Ray, I hope I'm wrong about this, but I don't think I am. I'm afraid to wait on this. He's deteriorating fast. Please call your dad."

"I will. Thank you."

"You're welcome. I look forward to hearing from you. Goodbye."

"I'll be in touch." The line went dead.

Ray put the phone in its cradle, leaned back in his office chair, and stared at the ceiling. *Lord, what does this mean? Please give us wisdom. Help my friend.*

⤞⤝

Ray sat across from Rhonda, his father, and Danielle. He glanced at Rhonda.

Her expression was wide-eyed, mouth open, obviously speechless.

"Are you OK?" Floyd asked.

Rhonda blinked. She glanced first to Ray, and then

to Floyd. "Yes," she said slowly. "But I'm just not sure I understand."

They exchanged looks.

"You need me to repeat—" Ray started.

"No, I heard you. I just don't think I believe it," Rhonda cut in.

Ray placed his hand on the edge of her tan coffee table and leaned forward. "Rhonda, you're a Christian woman. You read the Bible and you know what it says. This isn't as far-fetched as it sounds. James, I mean, Dr. Coulson, said—"

"I don't care what Dr. Coulson said, or didn't say. It's ridiculous!"

This had to be hard. No one could be expected to take this at face value.

Her face turned crimson, eyes mad with fear. "First, you come to me, and you say that the man I love is schizophrenic. That was difficult, I'll admit, but I bought it. Now this! You can't expect me to believe this!"

Ray cleared his throat. "But the Bible clearly talks about—"

"Look, I believe in the Word of God. *That* Book," she said, pointing to a worn, black Bible on the coffee table, "is my life saving grace. But things like that just don't happen anymore."

"Says who?" Floyd interjected.

Rhonda turned to face the elder man.

His glasses glimmered from the sunlight peeking through the blinds.

"I don't know, but I've never seen anyone—"

"Have you ever seen anyone bungee jump in person?" Floyd asked her.

"What?"

"Bungee jump. You know, where people tie ropes to their belts and jump off perfectly good bridges. Have you ever seen anyone bungee jump?"

"I don't know what this has to do with anything?"

"Indulge an old man, OK?" Floyd asked.

"No." She rolled her eyes. "No, I supposed I've never seen anyone bungee jump. So, what?"

"Well, then it must not happen."

"You're losing me."

Floyd leaned forward. "You said that we were crazy because you've never seen it happen. I'm simply pointing out that your logic is flawed."

"No. Your logic is flawed. There are pictures of people bungee jumping. There are stories of people who have done it and have lived to tell the tale. The same cannot be said about your theory."

"Do you believe the Bible?"

"Yes, we covered that."

"Then, you have your stories. And as far as people experiencing it in our lifetime"—Floyd looked at Ray, and then back to her—"If I'm right, Brian is proof that it still happens today."

31

Brian sat in his room afraid to shut his eyes. The beast visited him a lot more lately. He couldn't seem to shake the metallic sound of its voice. "You're mine."

No, he would not shut his eyes. Instead, he counted the tack marks on the wall. *There must be more than forty. Maybe I should get a poster.* He turned on his back and stared at the ceiling. This time he looked for shapes. His eyes burned, but he blinked to keep them open. He glanced around the vacant room and his gaze locked onto the Bible. Jake had read the Bible. Maybe he could pass the time that way.

Brian reached for the gold book on his nightstand, but something kept him from grabbing it.

"You're mine."

He squeezed his eyes shut, and then slowly opened them again. The room appeared empty.

"You *are* mine, Brian."

"Stop it!" Brian yelled to the vacant room, his eyes darting back and forth.

"Mine."

"Go away!" Brian grabbed his pillow and slammed it against his ears.

"You can't escape. You're mine."

Brian rolled back and forth. He hummed an old Beatles tune to drown out the voice.

"Mine! Mine! Mine!"

He jolted to his feet, rubbing his hands frantically

at his ears. Then paced. "Go away! Please, I beg you! Go away!"

"I can't do that, Brian."

"Who are you?"

"You don't remember?"

"No!"

Brian dropped to the floor, his ears raw with blood. He pinned his knees over his head and looped his hands over the back of his neck. And yet, the voice still came.

"I'm your master. I own you."

"But who *are* you?"

"You don't know?"

"No, just tell me!"

"You disappoint me, Brian. After all our talks, you still don't know me."

"You're a dream."

"No, I am Guilt."

Brian stood in the darkness, afraid to open his eyes. He could hear the beast laughing in the distance. Then Brian heard a familiar voice. A voice that did not belong to the hideous creature. He opened his eyes.

"Jake," Brian said. "How'd you get here?"

Jake waved his hand in the air and the darkness transformed into Brian's office. Jake crossed to the couch and plopped down. "I've always been here."

"Where *is* here?" Brian asked.

Jake laughed. He swung his boot up on the table. "On the couch."

"I don't understand. How'd we get back here?"

"I've always been here; in your mind, with your master. We're all connected. We are one."

"Who are *we*?"

"We are many."

"So there are more of you?"

"A few more."

Lara, Dr. Raven, and a ghostlike Krissy stepped from the shadows.

"We always come in sheep's clothing."

"But you read the Bible?"

Jake smirked. "There's only one name that I can't see or hear. King David is not one of them."

"But I don't understand." Brian stared at Dr. Raven. "You tried to help me. How could you be evil?"

"Our purpose was to deceive you. To keep *our* reality alive," Dr. Raven said.

"To drive you insane," Lara added.

"But why? What do you want from me?"

Jake crouched forward. Fiery red eyes glowed from his sockets. "Your death."

Brian trembled. He couldn't stop shaking. Everything went dark. Brian stumbled through the darkness. He reached out for a wall, but found none.

32

"Peace visits not the guilty mind."
(Nemo Malus Felix) Juvenal (55 AD-127 AD)

The three men sat silent in James' office.

Ray finally broke the peace. "Do you understand what we're telling you?"

"Well," James pulled his hands down his face. "I think you're saying that you believe my patient is demon possessed."

Ray nodded. "Yes, that's exactly what I'm saying."

The doctor shook his head. "This isn't 30 A.D. This is twenty-first century America. Things like that don't happen anymore."

"Now, you sound like Rhonda."

"Apparently Brian married himself an intelligent woman."

"Look, James." Floyd finally spoke. "I know it's hard to believe that it could happen here in the States, let alone in modern times, but it does happen. And I think we're seeing it for ourselves. Your dissertation was on schizophrenia, and even you admit that Brian's case is unusual."

James stared at his hands. "I would say it's more than unusual. It's a whole new disorder. I've never seen anyone like him before. One minute I think he has Dissociate Identity Disorder, the next he seems schizophrenic, other times he seems catatonic, and the next, just downright crazy."

Ray and Floyd exchanged smiles.

"I'm a godly man. You know this. But this is hard to swallow."

"Of course it is," Floyd said.

James stood and paced. "Supposing you're right, what do you suggest we do?"

"I would like to bring in a few people to intervene." Floyd walked to his side. "We could have a prayer meeting right in his room."

There was no way the hospital would allow that. "Sorry. That's not possible."

"Come on, James," Ray said.

"I'm sorry, no."

"Why not?" Floyd asked.

"Because I don't think I can get clearance for an exorcism in my hospital. After all, we're state funded."

"How many visitors can a person have?" asked Ray.

James stopped pacing and looked at Ray. "At the most? Five."

"Perfect."

"That still doesn't explain the intent of your visit. Besides, most visitors aren't allowed past the dining hall. And I don't think I can get clearance for casting out demons during breakfast."

"Ah, yes," Floyd placed his hands on his buddy's shoulders. "But patients have spiritual rights, am I right?"

"Yes, we always make the chapel available to them every Sunday morning."

"And if their spiritual needs are not being met?"

"Then we are allowed to bring in a rabbi or priest, or whatever their faith's clergy might be."

Floyd nodded. "Well, I propose that Dr. Brian Manifold's spiritual needs are not being met, and I recommend that we be allowed to bring in a pastor to meet those needs."

"With a small congregation, of course," Ray said with a mischievous smile.

"Yes, a mini church service," Floyd said.

"You both realize that you'll get me fired."

Ray laughed. "That's OK. If they fire you, I just so happen to have an opening on my staff."

"OK, fine," James laughed nervously. "I see that I'm out-numbered here. Sunday at 8:00 in the morning."

"Great." Ray clapped his hands once. "We'll be here."

❧

Sunday morning, an hour after breakfast, five visitors checked in at the Brighton Mental Hospital reception desk.

Danielle's heart beat fiercely. The thought of entering a "nut house" was not her idea of fun. When Ray called, and then Rhonda called, how could she possibly say no?

The receptionist handed each of them a visitor's badge.

The door buzzed open and Danielle's stomach soared into her throat. *Here we go.*

A man dressed in a doctor's coat, with kind eyes and a big smile, met them on the other side of the door. "Hello, I'm Dr. James Coulson. I'm your husband's counselor," he said, extending his hand to Rhonda.

She shook his hand and said timidly, "Nice to

meet you."

He offered her a reassuring smile, and then turned to the group. "Now, if you're sure you're all ready for this, please follow me."

The five of them made their way through a series of doors before stopping at a room marked 266.

Screams echoed up and down the hall, and her nose burned from the pungent smell of bleach. Danielle couldn't help but feel sad for Rhonda. The love of her life lived here.

The doctor shot Floyd and Ray a look before unlocking the door. "You only have four hours. Our guard, Nate, is a Christian, and has promised to cover for us. He actually believes your theory more than I do." Dr. Coulson stepped back and allowed them to enter.

Danielle's heart sank.

Brian lay on his bed rolling around in shredded linen.

Rhonda's eyes opened owl-wide.

"Aren't you going to tie him down?" Danielle asked.

Dr. Coulson frowned. "We did. He broke them. Twice."

Trembling, Danielle's legs locked, and she felt paralyzed.

Dr. Coulson walked to the door. "He's all yours." He smiled slightly, before he closed them in.

Danielle swallowed hard at the sound of keys locking them inside. What had she agreed to?

The pastor grabbed Danielle and Ray's hands. "Let's not waste any time. No fear. God is in control. Let's pray."

❧❧

"Make them leave, Brian," the beast hissed.

"No!" Brian yelled aloud.

"They can't have you. You're mine!"

"No! Never!"

"Yes, Brian. Ever since you killed your daughter. You've been mine."

"But I didn't kill her."

"Didn't you?"

"No!" Brian said. "Rhonda fell. It was only an accident. Just an accident."

"Yes, but who made her fall?"

"Did you hear me? I said it was an accident!"

"But you were drunk. Weren't you?" The demon circled him, sneering. "And that's what caused her to fall, wasn't it, Brian? Your drinking killed your baby. If you'd been sober, she never would have died. *You* killed her, Brian. Admit it. You murdered your own baby."

Brian flailed around and grasped his ears.

"Shut up!"

"And now you're mine. Mine!"

"No!"

"And soon you'll be ours for eternity."

"Never!"

The beast flinched.

Brian realized the creature's alarm.

"Why are you afraid of them?" Brian asked, pointing at the faces in the room.

"I fear nothing," the beast said.

"You fear their prayers."

❧❧

They prayed for almost three hours straight.

Danielle's head pounded, her body felt weak.

The pastor looked around at the faces, weary from the fight. "'A man who is loaded down with the guilt of human blood will run in fear until death,'" he said.

Rhonda looked at the pastor, her eyes swollen, her face red, but with a glimmer that suggested the Lord swelled her heart. "What?"

He shook his head and smiled. "I was quoting Proverbs 28:17."

"Say it again."

He repeated the scripture, "'A man who is loaded down with the guilt of human blood will run in fear until death.'"

A small tear crept down her cheek. "It's hopeless."

The pastor looked at the dejected man in the corner and shook his head. "Nothing is impossible for God. We simply can't give up."

"But we're running out of time."

He patted her shoulder. "Keep praying, dear. Your answer will come."

She bowed her head.

Danielle started to do the same.

The pastor moved toward Brian. He walked as close as he dared. He didn't touch him physically, but reached out a hand to the broken man. "God," he said, "we need a miracle."

The pastor spun around, rebuked the demon and Brian went limp.

෴

The beast let out a piercing scream and tore at Brian as something sucked the creature from the room.

Brian's chest constricted and he fell to the floor, heavy and wet from perspiration.

❧

Brian relaxed.

"Brian, how do you feel?"

"Like I've been beat up," he whispered to the man in front of him.

"In a sense, you have been." He helped Brian to the bed and pulled a chair next to him. "Do you remember me?"

"You're Pastor Van from my wife's church."

"That's right." He leaned forward. "We need to talk about what has happened."

"Now?" Brian asked, weakly.

"Yes, now." The pastor nodded to Ray and Floyd to help him sit up.

The rest of the group sat on the floor against the wall.

"Are you aware of what has been going on?"

"I'm schizophrenic," Brian answered.

"No, I don't think so."

Brian stared at the pastor.

"Rhonda tells me you both lost a child about six months ago. Is that true?"

Brian looked from Pastor Van to Rhonda.

She smiled.

He looked away. "Yes," he whispered.

"And you feel that you played a part in that accident?"

"I was the cause of it," Brian said.

"No... "Rhonda started to say, but the pastor shook his head. She closed her mouth.

"You must see that whether or not you were responsible for that accident is not what is important. What happens *now* is what matters."

Brian stared at him, but said nothing.

"Rhonda has already forgiven you. Now, you have to forgive yourself, and then ask God for forgiveness."

Brian looked away at the word *God*.

The pastor audibly took a deep breath. "We just spent the last three hours casting a demon out of your body."

"The beast," Brian said matter-of-factly.

"You believe me?"

"Yes."

"So, you believe in the devil, but do you believe in God?"

"He allowed this to happen."

The pastor glanced at Rhonda and motioned for her to continue praying.

Rhonda grabbed the hands of those around her and bowed her head.

"Brian, God helped your wife get through this. She lost her baby, and then her husband. It's God Who took care of your wife during those horrific times. Jesus cares about you, too. He wants so desperately to come into your heart. But first you have to admit your sin and ask Him to forgive you."

"I don't know if I can."

Rhonda spoke up. "I know you can."

Brian faced her.

She crossed to him and took his hand in hers. "You're alive and now we have a second chance."

A tear flowed from the corner of Brian's eye.

Rhonda squatted by the bed and lightly pressed her cheek against his. "It doesn't matter what we've done. Christ died for those sins. We have a chance because God loves us."

Brian closed his eyes. "It's so hard."

"Of course it is. Someone wants you to miss this opportunity, but I pray you won't. I love you. Jesus loves you. I want you to know what I know."

"But my guilt… "

Ray walked to the edge of the bed. "I watched the tapes from your office. Often you mentioned King David. You mentioned that he murdered to cover his guilt. But there is more to that story. The beauty of David's life is that God was willing to forgive him despite what he'd done. He even called David a man after his own heart." Ray smiled. "God doesn't hold grudges."

"That's right," the pastor added. "God throws all our transgressions into the sea of forgetfulness. You have the chance at true freedom."

The pastor wasn't saying anything Brian didn't know already. He had known for years that he should take this step. So, why was it so hard? It was funny that he had no problem making choices that practically destroyed his life, but when it came to making a commitment to Jesus, it was like swimming through mud. But he was exhausted and done running. His voice cracked, as he said, "OK."

The pastor leaned forward. "The first step, Brian, is to acknowledge that you're a sinner."

"That won't be hard."

Pastor smiled. "Next you have to believe in your heart that Jesus, God's Son, died for your sins and that He alone has the power to redeem you."

"I think I've always believed that. I just didn't want to accept it."

The pastor nodded. "Great. And lastly, you just need to ask Him into your heart."

Rhonda reached out and took his hand in hers. "I'm here."

"Just pray from your heart," James said and motioned for Rhonda to take his chair.

Rhonda sat down and squeezed Brian's hand.

"Do I have to pray out loud?" he asked, glancing around at each person in the room.

The pastor shook his head. "Only if you want to. God can hear you either way."

Brian closed his eyes. So much emotion poured over him. Broken and lost, he felt the need for God more than ever before. He spoke barely a whisper, "God, you see me. I'm a mess. But I can't do this anymore. Please come into my life. Forgive me of all of this. Starting with the pain I caused my family. Jesus, be my Savior from here on out. Amen."

As he raised his head, a huge grin crossed his wife's face.

"Amen," she repeated.

He kissed her hard, his body convulsed with tears of joy.

She hugged him back.

Peace enveloped him for the first time—he was happier than he could ever remember.

33

Danielle dragged her tired body outside the hospital, down the two-dozen steps, and to her car. All she wanted to do was sleep. What she'd just experienced was frightening, exhilarating, and completely exhausting.

"Leaving so soon?" Ray asked behind her.

With a hint of a smile, she flipped around and nodded.

"Not even saying goodbye."

She leaned against the front of her car and sighed. "You looked preoccupied. I didn't want to bug you."

"You could never bug me." He smiled, his entire countenance lit up. Never had he looked so attractive. Which was weird, since his hair was a mess and his eyes were bloodshot and tired.

"Really? That's not the signal you send me often."

He frowned. "I suppose that's fair."

Though she wanted to fix this with him, now didn't seem the appropriate time. She could barely keep her eyes open. "I need to get home and rest."

"May I drive you?"

She waved to her car. "Why? I'm right here."

"Because, honestly, I want to."

Man this guy is weird. She let out an exaggerated sigh and smiled. "Fine. But how will I get my car again?"

"I'll bring you back in the morning after I pick you

up for breakfast." He winked.

"Breakfast? I see." She stepped back and followed him to his car. "You do realize that we have work in the morning."

He held up a finger. "Ah, but here's the coolest part. We work at the same place."

"Yes, though I'm not sure how breakfast fits into all that."

He opened the car door for her, and then walked around to the driver's side. He turned on the engine and pulled out. "So, the drama is over."

Danielle's heart leapt. What did that mean? "The drama?"

"With Brian."

"You think so?"

Ray slowed at a yellow light. "I do."

"And?"

"And, I just thought—" He drove forward and turned onto the freeway.

"Yes?" *Just say it! You're killing me.*

"That I fear we won't see each other as much."

"Oh." Danielle turned her head to stare out the passenger window. She had her answer. It was over.

Rhonda had it all wrong. It wasn't Brian who kept Ray from committing, Ray just didn't want Danielle. Now that his excuse was gone, he knew he had to be honest.

She leaned her head against the glass and shut her eyes.

After a quiet drive, Ray drove in front of her apartment.

"Thanks." She got out and slammed the door closed.

Ray quickly got out, too.

Danielle turned and walked backwards. "You don't need to walk me in. You should get home and sleep."

"My mother would kill me if I didn't walk you to your door."

"Fine." She sighed.

They walked down the sidewalk, into the hall that led to her complex. When they reached her door, she pulled out her key and moved to unlock the door.

Ray caught her hand. His warm skin sent goose bumps up her arm. She was too tired to resist, to fight the feelings that threatened to take over.

"I meant it," he whispered.

"What's that?"

His eyes gazed into hers, less than an inch away. "That when the drama was over, I wanted you in my life."

Once again, Danielle felt disarmed. Her heart dropped into her stomach. "But in the car you said you'd see less of me. I don't understand you at all." She stepped back. "One minute you seem to be interested, the next you're...aah!" She flipped around, stuck her keys in the knob and turned.

Ray tugged her wrist, spun her back to him, and kissed her. Soft and inviting. His lips parted hers. After a moment, he pulled back and looked at her. "I mean it, Danielle. I want you in my life."

She blinked. "But why have you pushed me off?"

He brushed his lips against hers again. "Because if I'm in a relationship, I don't want anything to distract me. I couldn't give you my full attention with all I had to do with Brian."

She stared, unsure if he meant it. Would he turn back into Mr. Hyde?

"Say something," he said.

"I'm scared."

He stepped back and frowned. "Of me?"

"Of you changing your mind again."

He closed his eyes, pressed his lips together, and then opened his eyes. "I have liked you from the second we met. That has never changed."

Her eyes welled with tears.

"I kept pushing you away, because I knew it wasn't the right time. But my heart said differently. It was the hardest thing I ever had to do." Ray tucked a strand of her hair behind her ear. "I mean it. I don't ever want you out of my life again."

He touched his lips to hers again and her heart soared.

∂∾⋖

James entered the doorway of Room 266 just as Brian snapped his suitcase closed.

"So, you've heard the good news and are out of here?" James asked.

"Yes, Nate told me to pack an hour ago."

"Are you ready?"

Brian wasn't sure how to answer. *Ready?* He'd been outside reality for months. In the hospital, he didn't have to face it. "I think I'm a bit scared."

James nodded and walked next to him. "It's perfectly normal for patients to be apprehensive after a long stay. Can I help you carry anything?"

"No, I think I can manage."

"When is your wife getting here?"

Brian grabbed his bags and followed the doctor into the hallway. "She should already be here."

"Well then, let's not keep her." James smiled. "Number one rule for all men to remember. Never keep a beautiful woman waiting for you."

Brian returned his smile. He could see why Ray had sent him here.

They walked down the corridor and stood back, while James unlocked the doors. When they reached the reception station, Brian gulped a few chestfuls of air. "Here goes nothing."

"No, Dr. Manifold. Here goes life." James swung the door open.

Rhonda sat in the lobby. Her head shot up and a smile enveloped her face. She rushed to him, arms opened wide.

Brian grabbed her and held her tight. She put her lips to his, and he drank in her strawberry scent. Oh, how he'd missed her.

"Good-bye, Brian," James said. "Take care of yourself."

Brian peeked over Rhonda's shoulder. "Thank you, Dr. Coulson, for everything."

"My pleasure. Now get out of here before I have to explain rule number two." He smiled and shut the door with a loud bang.

Brian laughed.

"What did he mean by that?" Rhonda asked.

He shook his head. "Nothing."

"Well, I agree," Rhonda said. "Let's go home."

Epilogue

About Ten Months Later

"Good morning sunshine," Brian heard his wife say beyond the covers. He groaned and pulled the sheet to his nose. "What time is it?"

"Seven," she said. "Ray will be here soon."

He stretched his arm to encompass her head. "After today, I'll be able to apply for work."

"Are they really going to let you practice again?"

Brian kissed her temple. "I will have to be supervised for five years, but thanks to Ray and Floyd, I can help others again."

"Well, then you better get up. You don't want to miss that meeting with Ray." She nuzzled his neck.

"Keep doing that and I'm not going anywhere," Brian smiled.

She laughed. "OK, I'll get up so you can, too."

Brian rolled to his side. "Would you mind making some coffee? I need something to wake me up this morning."

"Not at all. Just get in the shower." She playfully pushed him out of bed.

"All right. I'm going." He kissed her nose and climbed out of bed.

Rhonda grabbed her robe and headed for the kitchen.

Brian walked into the bathroom and smiled. His

heart soared. Staring at his reflection, he felt a ridiculous amount of peace for all that they had endured. But the truth was, they were blessed.

∞∞

Ray pulled into the Manifold driveway and glanced at his new bride.

Danielle glowed.

"Have I told you how much I love you?"

"In the last hour, no."

He pulled her hand to his lips and kissed it. "Well, I do. With all my heart."

She giggled. "The feeling is mutual. Now you better go grab Brian, or we're all going to be late."

"Fine." He kissed her hand one more time, and then got out of the car.

The front door lay ajar. Ray stepped to the entrance and found Rhonda hugging the wall. "Are you OK?"

"Brian?" Rhonda yelled.

"What, dear?" Brian said from the kitchen.

"It's time!" she yelled back.

Ray's heart accelerated. He glanced back at the car.

Danielle smiled and motioned with her wrist that they were late. If only she knew.

He laughed.

Brian appeared in the hall. "I'm sorry, honey, what did you say? Time for what?"

"My water just broke," she said, joining him in the hall.

"Oh!"

"Hi," Ray said.

Brian glanced at Ray. "Oh, my ride."

Rhonda winced. "No, that's *our* ride. Let's go."

They hurried out the front door.

"Ray, you have impeccable timing," Brian said, helping his wife down the steps. "Would you mind chauffeuring my wife and me to the hospital? The baby's coming."

Ray laughed. "I'd love to. I wouldn't trust you to drive, anyway." He smiled at Rhonda and winked. "What do you think, Rhonda?"

"Onward," she said pointing out the door.

Ray and Rhonda laughed.

Brian playfully rolled his eyes.

Danielle got out and joined Rhonda in the backseat. Together, they worked through some sort of breathing exercises.

Despite his confidence, Ray drove like a maniac. He drove over a curb, ran two stoplights, and went at least twenty miles over the speed limit in street traffic.

"You'd think *you* were having the baby," Brian teased.

"It's like my sister is giving birth, OK?"

"You do know that uncles have to change poopy diapers," Brian joked, just as Ray sped through a fading yellow light.

Ray laughed. "We'll see."

When they pulled into the maternity wing, Rhonda's contractions were already five minutes apart. "Hurry or we're going to have this baby in the car," she moaned.

Ray peered at her in the review mirror.

She struggled to breathe through the pain.

He pulled into the emergency lane.

Brian and Danielle jumped out.

Danielle ran inside and returned a moment later

with a wheelchair.

They helped Rhonda in and then rolled her toward the entrance.

"I'll meet you inside," Ray yelled.

Brian waved over his shoulder and disappeared.

∂∞∂

"Excuse me," Brian said to the woman behind the front desk. "My wife is in labor."

The woman nodded and typed a few strokes on her keyboard. "Is she registered?"

Brian looked at Rhonda.

Rhonda nodded emphatically.

"Yes."

"Name?"

"Rhonda Manifold."

The woman typed a few more keys, and then said, "Yes, here she is. OK, just follow me."

"I'm going to wait for Ray," Danielle said.

"OK," Brian said.

The nurse directed them to a curtain at the far end of the lobby. She pulled a gown out of a drawer and handed it to Brian. "Have her change into this gown. Everything off. Someone will be with her in a moment." The nurse nodded and went back to the front desk.

Brian faced his wife.

Rhonda glowed.

He helped her into the white and blue-specked gown.

"I wonder if this is supposed to be in the front or the back." Rhonda asked, as she examined the opening in the gown.

"Back. You're going to want your epidural," Brian said.

Rhonda winked.

Brian helped her lay down in bed, and then kissed her forehead.

The doctor entered through the curtain and shook Brian's hand. "Dr. Manifold. I've read some of your research. Very intriguing." Then he turned to Rhonda. "Hello, Rhonda. Are you ready to have this baby?"

"Yes, doctor."

"Great. Let me just see if your baby is as ready as you are." The doctor adjusted the sheet so he could examine her. He clicked his tongue on the top his mouth. "Wow!"

"What is it?" Rhonda asked.

"I think you're ready to push."

"No," Rhonda said, "I haven't had my epidural yet."

The doctor laughed. "My dear, you're not going to need one. This baby will be out in no time. You're dilated to ten, fully effaced and the head is already crowning." The doctor pulled back the curtain and waved to the desk nurse.

"Yes, doctor?"

"Mrs. Manifold is ready. Please move her to a delivery room."

"Yes, doctor."

Brian helped Rhonda return to the wheel chair.

Her face contorted.

They followed the nurse down the hall to another room. This one looked private and comfortable. The nurse prepared Rhonda for delivery and left.

Brian leaned down to his wife and whispered, "I sure do love you."

She grimaced. "I love you, too." She breathed. "I think she's coming, and I'm not going to get my epidural."

Brian rubbed her arm. "I'm sorry about that."

The nurse came in again.

"Can you get Danielle? She's the blonde at the entrance," Rhonda asked to the nurse.

"I'll see what we can do." She left.

A moment later, Danielle ran in the door and kissed Rhonda's cheek. "I just heard that you're getting ready to push."

"Yes. Ow!" Rhonda grunted. "She's coming."

As if on cue, the doctor entered in a surgery coat and mask. "Ready?"

Rhonda nodded.

The doctor took his seat.

Three pushes later, Hope Manifold breathed her first bit of air. They laid her on Rhonda's stomach.

Brian cut the cord, a smile of fatherly pride smeared on his face.

The nurse took the baby to a plastic incubator, covered by a soft light.

Brian stared at her.

She was so perfect. So beautiful.

Ray entered the room and took in the scene. "Oh come on. I was only gone five minutes. Eight, tops."

Everyone laughed.

He walked to Danielle's side and interlaced his fingers with hers. "Someday we should do that," he whispered a bit louder than he probably intended.

"I'd love that," she said back.

The nurse turned with the swaddled baby. "Would you like to hold your daughter?"

"Are you kidding? I've been waiting a long time

for this moment." Brian took the fragile little lady from the nurse's arms, marveled, and then crossed to Rhonda and laid their baby in her arms. He leaned and kissed his wife's forehead.

"Thank you, honey."

"For what?" Rhonda breathed as she stroked their little Hope.

"For a second chance."

"I think you should thank God for that," Rhonda said.

"I do." He smiled.

Rhonda kissed his cheek.

Hope cooed.

They both looked down at her.

Brian caressed her tiny hand and smiled. "Welcome," he said, "to the rest of our lives."